# Fantastic Memories

MAURICE SANDOZ

# Fantastic Memories

 BOOKS FOR LIBRARIES PRESS
FREEPORT, NEW YORK

Copyright 1944 by Doubleday & Co., Inc.
First published 1957
Reprinted 1969 by arrangement

STANDARD BOOK NUMBER:
8369-3038-X

LIBRARY OF CONGRESS CATALOG CARD NUMBER:

70-85695

*To*
MISS ELIZABETH ARDEN
*who fought to make beauty eternal*

# Contents

| | |
|---|---|
| PREFACE | 11 |
| GRANDMAMA GLADYS | 15 |
| THE LIMP-PAGED ALBUM | 21 |
| A SLOW-MOTION CRIME | 27 |
| THE LADY OF THE CORNFLOWERS | 33 |
| THE POET | 43 |
| THE CRUTCHES OF UNCLE CELESTIN | 51 |
| SUSPICION | 57 |
| AT THE SPANISH CUSTOMHOUSE | 65 |
| FRIENDS | 73 |
| SOUVENIR OF HAMMAM MESKOUTINE | 83 |
| THE HAIRY HAND | 89 |
| ACCESSORY | 95 |
| IN THE CEMETERY AT SCUTARI | 105 |
| AN APPARITION | 113 |
| THE VISITATION | 119 |
| THE LEANING ROCK | 127 |
| THE LOVE-LETTER | 139 |

# Preface

AMONG those many unanswerable problems that haunt me there is one to which I willingly return. I ask myself whether the irresistible attraction that those fantastic beings, events, and things which, since childhood, have played so large a part in my life, now have for me is not due merely to their familiarity. Have they become a habit, perhaps, that I find difficult to give up? Or, on the other hand, has this very fascination drawn me unwittingly into the path of such singular and inexplicable coincidences?

This little book has but one merit in my eyes. It contents itself with the tale of strange happenings and makes no effort to explain them.

And that seems to me the best that can be done.

# Grandmama Gladys

*I* NEVER KNEW Grandmama Gladys. It would have been remarkable if I had, for she was my great-grandmother; but, as we invariably heard her alluded to by our parents as "Grandmama Gladys," we adopted the term ourselves, thus lightheartedly skipping a generation. In addition to which, as my father never failed to assure me, I should have gained nothing from the acquaintance of my grandfather's second wife, endowed though she was with an amazing beauty, retained till the day of her death. She was, according to his account, utterly indifferent to everything, animate or inanimate, that did not serve to embellish her life, in the process, incidentally, of embellishing herself.

She saw more of her hairdresser than her husband and spent ten times as much money on her perfumes as would have gone to the education of her two stepsons and her own daughter, the effect of whose birth on her figure she never quite forgave.

Grandmama Gladys was an Englishwoman, the only foreigner who figures in our family tree. I suspect her foreign origin to have been the main cause of the prejudice my parents showed toward her, for they were more Swiss in temperament than Helvetia herself. I am convinced that they would have been far more inclined to overlook the adorable creature's many eccentricities if she had hailed from Tessin or Les Grisons, instead of from the other side of the Channel, like one of those Rempler rose trees for which my parents had no great liking either. "Too many blooms and not enough scent," my father used to say.

The only child of a rich man who had been knighted in the reign of George IV, for "services rendered" (possibly a loan made to the Prince of Wales and tactfully forgotten), Gladys led as gay a life in London as was within the scope of a young girl of the age in which she lived. And this is saying a good deal, for in those halcyon days girls were permitted so little liberty that they ended by taking all!

She certainly did not lack admirers, "wooers," as they called them then. But, to the great distress of her parents, she turned a deaf ear to their sighs and refused them all in turn, in spite of the fact that some of them were highly eligible.

My great-grandfather, a young doctor, with two motherless sons on his hands, was summoned to the Court of St. James's to operate on the King.

His Majesty had refused to countenance anyone but Sir James Liverie, the court surgeon, but Sir James, having broken his arm, was unable to operate on his august patient and conceived the idea of sending to Switzerland for his most brilliant pupil, a young doctor whose reputation was already solidly established there.

The operation was a complete success. A ball was given in the Pavilion at Brighton to celebrate the King's recovery, and it was there that my great-grandfather first set eyes on the woman who was to become his wife.

He asked for an introduction, danced two polkas and a mazurka with her, fell, in his own words, "furiously in love," and told her so then and there—a declaration which was received with the icy coldness it deserved.

"*Une corbeille remplie de chardons d'Écosse*," he once said, "*et Dieu sait s'ils piquent, ces chardons écossais.*"

He was fated to meet Gladys again ten weeks later, in London this time.

To the intense surprise of everyone she abandoned the son of the Duke of Perth with whom she had been dancing, and came to meet him.

"Several months ago, Doctor, you paid me some rather exaggerated compliments," she began, with an inscrutable smile. "But perhaps you do not remember?"

"I have forgotten the sequel," was my great-grandfather's neat retort, "but, so far as the compliments are concerned, permit me to renew them."

She tapped him lightly on the lips with her fan and signed to him to follow her to a more secluded spot. Here she turned and faced him.

"You declared, if I remember right, that you found me 'perfectly beautiful,'" she reminded him.

"All the same, if you had looked at me with the professional eye of a doctor, instead of with the indulgence of an admirer, you would no doubt have perceived that my eyes do not match!"

Examining her critically for the first time, my great-grandfather became aware of the fact that there was indeed a flaw in the beauty he had considered above reproach.

"You have no cause for anxiety," he assured her, after a brief scrutiny. "Your eyes are perfectly symmetrical. The fault lies with your eyelids, which are not quite of the same length."

"Do you mean to say that the trouble can be remedied?" cried Gladys eagerly, laying her hand on his arm.

He thrilled at her touch.

"I will not say that I hope, but that I am quite certain that I can remodel the eyelid," he declared.

No more was said, but two days later my great-grandfather received an invitation from his future father-in-law, and shortly afterward, to the astonishment of everyone, the widower married the beautiful Gladys and bore her away from the town in which she had been so much admired. He operated on her eyelid, delivered her from the only real care she had ever known, and became, for the rest of his life, the most unhappy of men.

The story concerns my own people. Taste forbids me to speak more plainly.

# The Limp-Paged Album

I HAVE ALREADY spoken of my great-grandfather. Doctor, surgeon, chemist, botanist, perhaps even something of a sorcerer, he would certainly have been burned at the stake, or died on the rack had he lived a century earlier.

He worked for choice in the hospitals in the big seaports. These offered a rich field for research. "One found everything there, even leprosy," he declared once, rubbing his hands with an air of rapture. He passed his nights in recording his observations, surrounded by retorts, crucibles, human skulls, and strange instruments. The censorious talked below their breaths of impiety, insensibility, even of sacrilege.

Among his legacies to us is an old album. It is distinctly shabby and of vast dimensions. I still cling to it, for it reminds me of my childhood.

Those sufficiently curious to open it will be astonished, to begin with, by the small number of its pages—twelve, to be exact. Then they will be disappointed by the quality, with one or two exceptions, of the pictures. But if they be observant, or, better still, imaginative, they will remain fascinated by this collection, in which everything seems calculated to surprise them.

The thickness of the pages is unusual and their odd limpness disconcerting to the fingers that turn them. They curl back on themselves like the buckskin that is still used in the burnishing of gold.

But the most potent quality of this album is the softness, the actual warmth of its pages. I have found myself holding them to my face, closing my eyes and wondering whether I was not pressing my cheek against that of a human being. And that impression was so strong that I could almost catch the sigh of a quick breath or the faint beat of a heart.

As for the pictures themselves, in spite of a similarity of technique they are certainly the work of various amateurs and the subjects have no logical continuity.

The first page bears the image of a pagoda. It is well drawn and towers, nine stories high, between two curious suns, in relief, whose presence is not at first easily explainable.

The second drawing, less able, represents in monotint the head of a woman. Her hair looks more like a bunch of black grapes than one of the chignons then in fashion. From either side of the coiffure little chains hang in the manner of earrings. They culminate in two baroque pearls, these also represented by two curious little reliefs. Anyone running a finger over the page is immediately conscious of them and recaptures suddenly a sensation that will not be new to him, though for many, if not all of us, it remains unexpected and unaccountable.

The other drawings are too mediocre in quality to be worthy of mention, but the last, the twentieth, is interesting.

It is of the life-size head of a tiger, in three colors, orange-tawny, blue-black, and crimson, this last color being reserved for the gums and the corners of the eyes.

My father did not like to see us fingering these curious pages.

"Leave that book alone, children," he would say, frowning, and he would press on us a volume full of brightly colored plates illustrating the flora of the Dutch Indies. For a moment we would be dazzled by the fruits and flowers, but, hardly had he turned his back than, very quickly, we returned to our first love, the mysterious book and the face of the woman who wore the strange earrings.

A connoisseur, looking at the head of the tiger, would immediately be reminded of the art of the Far East. But, if he were to examine the ferocious mask more closely, the tippling of the outlines and, particularly, of the shadows, would put him on the scent.

"Tattooing!" he would exclaim, pushing the book aside in disgust.

And, in fact, they are tattoos. The album consists of twelve pieces of human skin, taken from the chests of twelve sailors who had died in hospital!

But do not blame the originator of this macabre collection too hurriedly.

# THE LIMP-PAGED ALBUM

What my great-grandfather was in search of was the secret of eternal youth. For years he worked, untiringly, desperately, to conserve the beauty of the woman who was his all, and to whom he meant so little. Grandmama Gladys departed this life at the age of seventy, radiantly beautiful, with her cohort of admirers as large as ever, though for half a century Death had done his best to thin their ranks.

I understand now why my father did not like to see us poring over that album.

We did not know when we bent over the face of the woman with the strange headdress that the pearls in her earrings were formed by the nipples of the flat breast of a sailor lad who had died in hospital.

# A Slow-Motion Crime

WHILE EVOKING the image of my father it seems natural to relate here the story of an event in which he was concerned and which made a great impression on my brothers. But as my parents were, very naturally, afraid of the effect stories of this nature might have on an imaginative and impressionable child, I did not hear of it till much later.

It was during the autumn of 1897. While my mother and I were enjoying a holiday on the shores of the Lake of Constance, my father invited certain Alsatian friends of his, sportsmen like himself, to lunch at the house of Grandmama Gladys.

I imagine the tales of sport must have kept them lingering over the meal, for by three o'clock in the afternoon they had not left the table, and one of the guests having begun to boast, with the assurance of a connoisseur, of the brandy of his country, my father decided that he was worthy of a certain burgundy that ordinarily he offered only to a very favored few. To this end he sent Margaret, the young parlormaid, to the cellar, ordering her to bring "one of the three bottles without a label that she would find together in the left-hand corner, to the left of the door as she went in." I quote his exact words, which I have just reread in the reports of the Tribunal of Police in the Canton of Neuchâtel.

The girl obeyed his instructions. After some time, as she did not come back, my eldest brother was sent to fetch her.

He did not return either.

My father became not only impatient, but anxious. He asked his friends to excuse him and departed for the cellar himself.

Again some time elapsed. The guests, in their turn, beginning to feel apprehensive, were thinking of pursuing their host when they heard the sound of heavy footsteps ascending the cellar stairs. A door opened, but did not shut again, as though the person who had passed through it were hampered by a heavy burden.

Then they became aware of another noise, that of a body being deposited on the divan in the hall, followed by the shrill cries of a woman in the throes of an attack of nerves. Through the window they could see my brother running, bareheaded, across the garden in the direction of the road. At last my father returned, pale and very agitated. He had sent his son to the nearest police station. A horrible crime, he said, had been committed in our cellar.

Then he related what had happened.

On entering he had observed, by the light of a taper, his eldest son trying to raise the prostrate form of Margaret from the ground. My father saw that she had fainted and realized almost at once what had affected her.

Behind the big-bellied flagon she had pushed aside, lying on the ground, within easy reach of her hand, was the freshly severed head of a man!

During this recital Margaret, in a voice broken by sobs and cries, never ceased to reiterate that she had recognized the head as that of the postman who served our district.

"How could you expect me not to recognize him?" she moaned, with a naïveté that was revealing.

The police were represented by the *Juge d'Instruction* in person, supported by a couple of stout fellows who showed no inclination to investigate the scene of the crime. They were obliged, however, to accompany him when he descended the stairs.

Without hesitating he took the head in his hands, felt it, smelt it, carried it up into the daylight, and then, perplexed, stood for a long time scratching his own poll.

Suddenly his hands went back to the eyes of his ghastly burden. He tapped them with his finger and burst into a hearty laugh.

Everyone stared at him in astonishment. Anxious glances were exchanged. Had the judge's mind given way?

"It is an anatomical subject!" he exclaimed at last, between gusts of laughter. "An admirable one, but look, the eyes are artificial. They are made of glass!"

# A SLOW-MOTION CRIME

Everything was explained. This new trophy was but another victorious tribute to the science of the husband of Grandmama Gladys.

With a skill with which even the embalmers could not vie, he had succeeded in making the head of this unfortunate dead man incorruptible yet conserving all the flexibility of the living tissue. The relic is now carefully preserved in the Musée de Médecine of one of our native universities. Even today one can pinch the cheeks and part the pale lips. Only the eyes had lost their brilliance, and it was for this reason that this remarkable doctor had elected to replace them with glass. Then, not knowing what to do with so embarrassing an object, which he realized might not only terrify his children but prove something of a shock even to the insensible Gladys herself (though here he need have had no misgivings), he had hidden this anatomical specimen worthy of a waxworks museum behind his stock of burgundy.

It was calculated to reappear, with dire consequences, when the ranks of the bottles became depleted. But it was fifty-five years before the revelation took place, and it is more than possible that at least some of the praise that was accorded to my great-grandfather's work was due to the depth and profundity of our cellar!

The day after this emotional interlude Fridolin, our postman, made his customary appearance. If I may be allowed to close this sinister story on a lighter note I should like to say that, though Fridolin had kept his own head, Margaret, poor wench, had completely lost hers and could see nothing but him, everywhere and always!

# The Lady of the Cornflowers

*I*N A preceding story I have spoken of the wisdom my father had shown in keeping from me the emotions which shook the entire household when the "newly severed" head was discovered in the cellar.

He could hardly have foreseen that, some months later, in circumstances which it was impossible to anticipate, I was to undergo a violent nervous shock. The reader will appreciate this when he has heard the story of the Lady of the Cornflowers.

My father and mother were both passionately fond of travel, and that at a time when the majority of people did not transport themselves readily unless it was for reasons of health or business.

That year, 1896, if my memory holds good, it was Egypt, or at any rate North Africa, which had tempted my parents from their home. I do remember that my mother returned from the journey with a gingerbread complexion that both fascinated and distressed me. I think I had a suspicion that she had been changed in some way during the journey.

During these long absences I was terribly lonely. My brothers, older than myself, were languishing in pseudo-English boarding schools in the then-prosperous Lausanne and I was left alone with my nurse, Fanny, a peasant from the mountains, a still vigorous old woman of the highest principles when occasion demanded. We were then living on the shores of the Lake of Constance, on an estate so far away from the nearest town that unexpected visitors never disturbed us.

The reader will appreciate my delight when, after three months passed in the monotonous society of Fanny, she came into the little room that served as my bedroom bearing a mauve envelope addressed to me.

In those days I could have counted on my fingers the letters I had received. Never had one of such a fascinating color or written on such elegant paper come my way! In those days I must have been something of a snob and appreciative of such details.

But what was still more glorious about that envelope was the seal—a great, gooseberry-colored blob! I am not sure that I did not lick it, in the hope of combining the pleasures of both tongue and eye!

On the shining surface of the wax were two lions, rampant, wearing crested helmets. Real lions that I have seen since have always seemed to me but poor relations of these, inferior and meretricious.

I could hardly believe my eyes.

"Is it for me? Really my own?" I demanded of Fanny.

She nodded and, with the aid of one of her hairpins (I wonder whether those black, sturdy hairpins still exist? They were formidable weapons, more suggestive of barbed wire than anything else), she opened the envelope, not only without tearing it, but, to my great joy, leaving the seal intact.

It was she who read me the letter, for I was more familiar in those days with print than handwriting, and even today am the most illegible of scribes.

Madame de Bellerive, a friend of my mother's, begged to invite Monsieur Maurice Sandoz (and she even addressed him in the third person singular!) to go to tea with her at four o'clock on the following Wednesday at the Château de Hirtzheim.

"I shall have to iron your sailor suit," sighed Fanny, for she looked upon best clothes as objects to be admired but not worn, and embalmed them in a mixture of pepper, camphor, and naphthalene, a triple bouquet the odor of which still takes me back to festive occasions in the past.

That night I slept badly. My strange dreams, colored by the anticipation of my visit to the Château de Hirtzheim, filled the short intervals of slumber.

Dawn seemed unusually slow in coming, for time appears to change its cadence for those who hope or suffer. At last! At last! I heard the strident voice of a cock; another clarion call answered from a distance. The moon suddenly looked silly, because she still showed herself when she was no longer needed.

Then came the first rays of the sun and, at last, the longed-for apparition of Fanny, bearing the strangely odorous suit.

Oh, that sailor suit! Its cap was adorned with a legend in gold: *The Intrepid*, and its tunic with a completely aphonic whistle, suspended ironically from a massive cotton halyard.

Fanny hastened to warn me that I was not to put on this brilliant uniform till two o'clock in the afternoon, otherwise she would have ironed it in vain.

I was impatient and at a loose end. What was I to do with myself? I pretended to study the inexplicable vagaries of English spelling, every five minutes consulting the tortoise-shell clock on my mother's writing table.

At lunch I swallowed an egg which seemed to me as large as an ox, so constricted with impatience was my throat. After that I nearly strangled myself with an apple.

At last it was time to dress, under the eagle eye of Fanny. Then the cabin boy of the *Intrepid* made his way to the jetty and thence to the steamer, vaguely humiliated at being accompanied, both coming and going, by a faithful old nurse, who had no opinion of his wisdom or discretion. And, as will be seen, she was not far wrong.

I refused to look at the charming view which unrolled itself before my eyes. My whole attention was fixed on the horizon and my only ambition was to sight the two turrets of the Château de Hirtzheim.

They appeared at last, increasing with my impatience as we approached the landing stage and I jostled the other passengers in my efforts to be the first to set foot on dry land, much to the distress of Fanny, who blushed for my manners.

When I had arrived at the château my enthusiasm waned. It did not please me at all to be one among a hundred, and I could see a crowd of small girls and boys playing in the garden. In those days I had a craving for distinction of which the years have cured me.

Another disappointment! Madame de Bellerive decided in favor of round dances, and from that day to this I have never cared to clasp the, usually damp, hands of my fellow creatures for long—an obligation inseparable, as we all know, from the performance of round dances.

And the inane words that went with them! They revolted me! Here is an example:

> *"A thin stick to beat down nuts,*
> *I will not say who this may be.*
> *Kiss, kiss,*
> *And we shall see."*

The verse is halting and the rhymes poor, a poetic "Cour de Miracle."

But I could have borne the deplorable doggerel. What exasperated me was the obligation to kiss and allow myself to be kissed for no reason whatever.

The meal that followed at five o'clock reconciled me to life once more, and certain chocolate meringues are still a glorious memory. There were strawberry meringues, but, no doubt on account of their tender color, they seemed to me fit only for girls, and I refused with the utmost determination to taste them, in spite of a longing I could hardly suppress.

Finally the game which was organized after this repast restored my happiness completely. The absence of Madame de Bellerive was one of the elements in this discovery. I may add that, to my relief, this game did not entail either songs or kisses.

It was called "The Black Beast" and consisted of a sort of inverted "Hide and Seek." One player hid while the others tried to find him.

One serious failing I noticed in the "Black Beasts" who succeeded each other: they lacked imagination in the choice of a hiding place. A few minutes of search, ten at the utmost, and the "Beast" was taken in its lair, crouched behind the trunk of a tree, only partly hidden in a clump of bamboo, or huddled in the shade of a stone seat.

"If my turn comes to be the 'Black Beast,' " I thought to myself, "I'll hide so well that no one will find me!" And I pictured myself buried under a heap of dead leaves or crouched in the depths of the dog kennel, both of them godsends in my eyes.

And, would you believe it? My turn came almost at once. Public favor, or disfavor, singled me out for the role of the "Beast."

I approached the dog kennel. It was occupied by its legitimate proprietor, a colossus whose red eyes did not appeal to me.

# THE LADY OF THE CORNFLOWERS

I made for the heap of dead leaves and proceeded to scoop out armfuls of decayed vegetation with which to cover myself.

Myriads of Centipedes, vulgarly known as wood lice, swarmed in the cavernous depths of the mound and, with that unconscious duplicity that the child so constantly uses toward himself, I told myself emphatically that I would never grieve my dear Fanny by dirtying my sailor suit. It was so beautiful!

The leaves really were too filthy! But time was passing. I must find a refuge. I ran into the park.

There I found a curious structure, a low, rectilineal building, the axis of which was oddly indicated by a little tower, and which, it seemed, was partly buried, as though it had been built on an unusually deep foundation. It was an orangery.

The door gave under my hand and I entered.

It was spring, and all the oranges, in their tubs, now occupied the place of honor on the terrace of the château.

I went down ten steps into a huge and completely empty room. The noise of my feet resounded, awakening strange echoes, which I found very disquieting. I gained a certain reassurance from the fact that I could envisage the room at one glance, that it was empty, and that I must be, therefore, in consequence, the only author of these odd noises.

Though reassured I felt uneasy, for in this room there was no concealment for me anywhere. My pursuers had only to enter the orangery to find me at once. Then I saw, facing me, let into the wall, exactly in the center between two buttresses, a narrow door. I approached it on tiptoe, so as not to reawaken the echoes.

My spirits fell. The door was locked. I shook it with all my strength, but in vain. Then I remembered a dodge of our gardener's when a door, usually that of the cellar, refused to open. I put my shoulder to it, hurling myself against it in an attempt to force it.

But at my age and with my sparrow's bones the gesture was little more than symbolic. Though it relieved my feelings, or rather their intensity, I could not pretend that it was effective.

It had, however, one immediate result. I felt a sharp pain on the top of my head and realized a moment later what had caused it. An enormous key bounced off my cranium and struck the ground.

It had been balanced on the narrow lintel of the door, and though my efforts had not had any effect on either the panels or hinges, they had at least succeeded in dislodging the key from a hiding place in which I should never have dreamed of looking.

I was attacked by scruples. Had I the right to use this key that had fallen from heaven?

My conscience immediately supplied the answer. I had no right. So, hoisting myself on tiptoe, I made several vain efforts to replace it in its hiding place.

Then, outside, I heard the voices of my playmates. After all, had I not sworn to discover a place where they could not find me? Fate had come to the rescue. Should I not be a fool to refuse her aid?

I pushed the key into the lock and gave it a turn. The door did not budge. I turned the key a second time and the door opened.

I stopped, petrified.

I found myself standing on the threshold of a small room, illuminated only by an oval skylight, and full, so it seemed, of a sort of opal mist. The last rays of the sun, striking through the narrow window, pierced this odd atmosphere, forming a cone-shaped beam, such as is seen when light crosses a layer of air charged with vapor, or a room full of smoke. And the culminating point of this beam touched and illumined the strangest apparition I had ever set eyes on.

Dressed in an electric-blue dress and seated erect on a pouffe upholstered in pastel blue was a lady.

She was old; the white hair that showed beneath her ruched bonnet told me this. In her right hand she held a book. I had evidently interrupted her while reading.

In front of her, on a little shelved table of green marble, was a bouquet composed of ears of barley, blades of oats, and blue cornflowers. In spite of my emotion I noticed that these flowers were artificial.

For some seconds there was silence, but soon it became intolerable.

"I beg your pardon, madame," I stammered, my heart beating as though it would burst. "I did not know—I did not mean——"

My voice died away, strangled in my throat.

The old lady continued to stare at me, and that look, passing over the top of the book she held in her hand, pierced and transfixed me, as if I were something at a great distance. She seemed to see into me and through me, as though my body were transparent.

I could stand it no longer. I fled.

Who could she be, this old woman, richly dressed, who sat reading, alone, in this little enclosed space, and of whose presence there was no sign in the deserted outer room?

I ran through the orangery, the echo filling it with a tumult of footsteps that only served to increase my terror. Outside the others were looking for me, but the moment I appeared they ran away as fast as their legs would carry them, calling out: "Black Beast! Here's the Black Beast!" with the result that I found myself alone at the very moment when I could least bear solitude. Then I gave way to panic. I was no longer the "Black Beast." The real Beast was behind me, in the orangery, but it was an electric-blue beast and it ran after me. It would catch me . . .

My frantic course carried me to the château, where my arrival made a fine sensation. I sobbed, shivered, was livid, and unable to utter a word.

Fanny put an end to the painful scene by carrying me off as quickly as possible and pushing me into the first boat for Constance.

I was now safe and I knew it. In spite of which all that night I never ceased to shiver. Nothing would stop this nervous trembling, neither caresses, promises, nor threats. Nothing, not even the incredibly nasty valerian which was forced down my protesting throat.

My emotion outlived my fright. When my parents came back, directly the customary greetings were over, before, even, I had examined the presents they had brought me (though I remember a piece of sugar cane well worthy of my attention), I poured out in one breath the account of my extraordinary adventure. But I told the story very quickly and badly, the artificial cornflowers got mixed up with the curls of the old lady and the beam of light with her baleful regard.

"The child is mad," my father declared, when he found himself alone with his wife. "I always dreaded this and now I need dread it no longer. He has completely lost his wits."

"All the same, I think it might be as well to question Marie de Bellerive," suggested my mother gently. "In spite of everything there must be some foundation for that nightmare he has been describing."

They acted accordingly, with the result that my father's fears were laid to rest. I had not lost my wits. He could not forgive himself for the injustice he had done me, but he waited for several years before repeating to me the conversation he had had with Madame de Bellerive.

This is what she told him. Her grandmother, the wife of a celebrated general, feared death less than the tomb and the things that happened in it.

To putrefy beneath the earth was, in her eyes, an insult to the human body, more particularly to hers. Better she said, to be "eaten of worms" alive, like Herod, than to furnish their meal after death.

And as she realized that, in spite of pills and doctors, she would have to die one day, she made her heirs promise to place her, directly after her death, in a jar of alcohol, after the manner of preserving rare specimens in the collection of reptiles that she had admired in the museum.

Her son-in-law, respecting her last wishes, but opposed to the idea of a jar, merely bricked up the tower of the orangery, after depositing inside it with full ceremonial his defunct mother-in-law, adding the accessories I have described. He had then submerged her in several tons of alcohol.

Two crystal walls sealed both the door that gave access to the tower and the skylight through which, every twenty years, many liters of fresh spirits were poured.

At the time of my adventure the stale alcohol had become opalescent; the eyeballs of the Lady of the Cornflowers, grown a little stale herself, in spite of the alcohol, had become discolored and, a detail which had done much to increase my terror, the whole of the eyelashes of her left eye had slipped on to the center of her cheek. As for the glass, its perfect transparency rendered it invisible. The whole effect was calculated to frighten more valiant people than myself.

Even today, after a lapse of forty years, I prefer not to dwell on the appearance of the Lady of the Cornflowers.

And the reader may be grateful to me.

# The Poet

**T**HIS AFTERNOON," said my mother, "a pianist and a poet are coming to tea. Whatever you do, do not suggest that the pianist should play. This is his first visit and it would be in the worst possible taste."

I must admit that this warning struck me as quite superfluous. Did not I, twice a week, have to sit for one solid hour on a hard and wabbly stool, beside Madame Froebel, being admonished to "mind my thumb" and "mark the time firmly" on the yellow keys of an ancient piano? And Madame Froebel, overconscientious, was in the habit of giving precisely sixty minutes in return for a ticket inscribed "one hour."

If my lesson was considered to have gone well Madame Froebel, as a reward, would sit down to the piano and play, better, I must admit, than myself, "The Merry Peasant," and Heller's "Berceuse," the pieces which I then happened to be studying.

And as I had good reason to know every note of these compositions it gave me no pleasure to hear them played and never, no, never, would it have occurred to me to extend so rash an invitation to the expected visitor. It seemed to me inevitable that he would burst into the "Berceuse" or "The Merry Peasant." I was somewhat surprised that my mother had not admonished me in the same fashion with regard to the poet, but the omission only served to prejudice me in his favor, and from the moment he arrived, I adopted him, to the exclusion of the pianist. The latter struck me as boorish, while the poet impressed me with his supreme elegance.

His hands in particular fascinated me. Their polished nails shone like dewdrops; they might have been mirrors for skylarks and no wonder that a young starling like myself fell for them at once.

His face certainly showed the pallor and gravity which I realized could belong only to a poet.

Being anxious to ingratiate myself with this disciple of Apollo, I never ceased to press the sugar basin on him, and no doubt for fear of hurting my feelings, he accepted lump after lump. Poor poet! He drank syrup that day, but I was in a seventh heaven.

"Monsieur," I ventured timidly at last, when he had put down his cup, "how does one write poetry?"

With an air half serious, half joking, he said: "You need for that a *Dictionary of Rhymes*, plenty of cigarettes, and about ten years' serious study of the classics."

A gloom seemed to settle over my future. I could, at a pinch, ask for a *Dictionary of Rhymes* as my next birthday present, I might even succeed in appropriating my father's cigarettes, but ten years of classical study seemed to me unsurmountable.

The two visitors departed and I was left dreaming.

But I burned to see the poet again. I succeeded, and I do not think he was displeased to hold forth to such a fervent and attentive listener. It is a fact that very few people dislike being listened to religiously.

He it was who really taught me to read and write. I am not alluding to the mechanical actions we learn at school, but to the power to read slowly, with attention, striving to visualize, down to the most intimate detail, those images that the author tries to evoke. He taught me to analyze, first by ear, then by sight, the harmony that flows from a happy phrase.

If I reserve a place for the poet in these recollections it is not from gratitude for the many true, precise, and useful things he taught me. No, it is because he gave me the key of gold that opens the doors of imaginary palaces and because he made me at home in their capricious labyrinths, where he taught me to wander about but never lose myself.

One afternoon in September, not long after our first meeting, the poet deigned to visit our garden, which he had not yet seen and which I was only too proud to exhibit.

Instead of bread and salt, those symbols of hospitality, I proposed to offer him a ripe and absolutely perfect pear, the only fruit of a tree that I had planted with my own hands, the dirty hands of a little gardener, three years before.

# THE POET

It was the first fruit of a ducal tree (a "Duchesse" pear tree). In offering it to the poet I was voluntarily sacrificing my greed, my curiosity, and three years of impatience on the altar of my admiration.

The poet contemplated the pear which hung, motionless, at the end of a branch that bowed beneath its weight.

"No, do not pick it now," he said. "We will come back for it in an hour. By that time it will have attained all the attributes of perfection."

I was, I must admit, very much astonished. But as such desires counted as orders I obeyed, quite at sea as to how the passage of one hour could influence the qualities of an already ripe and beautiful pear.

I introduced my friends the plants and flowers to my friend the writer. I showed him the Calycanthus, which gives out an aroma of strawberries over an area of a hundred meters; the aromatic turpentine; the Wellingtonia, which five people, with their arms extended, could not span. I presented to him our cedars, our chestnuts, our copper beeches, and a host of others. All these I paraded before the no-doubt-rather-bored eyes of the master to whom for the moment I had elected to act as mentor.

At the end of a long hour a turn in the path brought us once more to the pear tree.

I picked the fruit and handed it to my companion.

"Tell me, monsieur," I said (I continued to address him in this way for several months, for it did not seem to me that anything would ever authorize me to address a poet by his Christian name), "tell me, please, why you like that pear better now than you did some time ago?"

"When we came this way an hour ago," answered the poet, "the tree was in shade and its fruit hanging inert and frozen, a lifeless thing. Now it is bathed in sunlight. Place it against your cheek. Don't you feel as if you were pressing another cheek, warm as your own? Now, with every particle of that fruit I shall taste a little of that sun that bestows its rays so charily in this terrible region of ours, which, for reasons that I cannot pretend to understand, we have christened the Temperate Zone."

It was thus, in a garden, at the close of a beautiful day, that the poet showed me one of those secret paths that are sometimes sought for for so long by those who seek perfection in the art of living.

I was destined to visit him a year later, in Paris. It was at the beginning of October and I was with my parents, who had decided to spend the autumn in Brittany.

I was obsessed less with the prospect of seeing the sea for the first time than with that of at last visiting the home of a poet. And I was not disappointed.

An ivy-covered court separated the house from the road, stifling and deadening all sounds from without.

To my great joy I discovered that the traditional bell had been replaced by a knocker. It was made, if I remember clearly, in the form of a satyr and one had to lift him up by the horns, or possibly pull his beard, to make him fulfill his office.

The door gave on to an antechamber hung with tapestries, bearing orange and lemon trees growing in dark green tubs and embellished with fruit and birds.

Then came the drawing room, divided up by screens in Japanese lacquer. Little tables and fragile chairs were dotted here and there.

These articles of furniture seemed to me so delicate and frail that my admiration for the poet who could live among them without breaking anything increased.

In the middle of the room hung a Venetian chandelier of opal glass. It floated in the silence like a gigantic jellyfish. The felt carpet fascinated me almost as much as the chandelier. It seemed to me to be woven with those azure butterflies known as the Argus, whose wings bear a large blue eye, wide open on the summer sun.

Against the wall, to right and left of a black marble fireplace, long, narrow mirrors faced other mirrors of the same shape, and, reflecting each other, formed dream galleries which seemed to go on to infinity.

The master of the house did the honors. He showed me a peasant kitchen which served as his dining room, and which, at the moment, was in the sole possession of a green parrot.

He also showed me his bedroom, almost entirely occupied by an immense bed. I particularly admired the canopy, the corners of which were royally adorned by four ostrich plumes.

Above the cushions which ornamented the bed by day the wall was decorated with a trophy. Looking back I can still see those ancient instruments, arranged in a sheaf. A guitar in the form of a lyre, a mandolin, a viola d'amore, and a shepherd's flute decorated with ribbons. I almost forgot the tambourine with its tiny gold cymbals. No doubt this orchestra lulled the sleeping poet's dreams with sweet harmony.

No, I was not disillusioned. And yet, toward the end of my visit I was conscious of a slight chill. Outside, it was raining softly. The light was gray. The corner of the sky that one could see over the ivy clustered round the window was cinder-colored. Everything spoke of autumn.

"I do not like October," I said to the poet. "It's the first month that makes me think of winter."

"You will love October in the days to come, when you are tired of the bright colors which blind one in summer. But, as you regret the summer so much, I will bring it back to you."

He had risen and was pulling down long, lemon-yellow blinds over the windows.

"It is better already," he said, indicating with a gesture the illusion of sunshine that had suddenly pervaded the room, "but we can improve on it. They say, from laziness or cowardice: 'Striving to better, oft we mar what's well,' which is merely a way of saying that it wasn't really 'well' in the first instance."

With these words he descended to the court and closed the outside shutters, in such a manner as to leave a space between them only as large as the palm of one's hand.

The effect was magical. In contrast to the dusk already achieved in the room the blinds, in the tiny spaces that were lighted from outside, gave out that ardent note they would have struck had a pitiless sun been shining on the windows. It seemed as if the shutters had been hastily closed to keep out the heat and glare of an August day.

The poet placed a bouquet of red roses in the path of one of these rays. It was just another bit of summer introduced into the scene. But even then my new friend did not seem quite satisfied.

He took from the chimney piece a little cardboard box and shook it with an air of mystery.

"Here is summer," he said. "Here, at last, is summer."

And he opened the apparently empty box.

At once the room was alive with the buzz of flying bees.

For an instant they filled it with their humming. Then there was a sudden shock, a double or triple impact against the windowpane. Bewildered, they stopped. A silence of two seconds, then they flew to the other end of the room, only to return and hurl themselves once more against the window, drunk with the false beams of the sun, a mirage evoked by the fantasy of a poet!

And that humming, that repeated impact against the window, brought back those lovely vanished days so perfectly that, when my host asked me to choose, I took a glass of lemonade instead of tea.

"He's a magician," I thought, "like the ones in the fairy tales."

Years passed. I followed the advice of the poet. I even arrived sometimes at a comprehension of the technique of his simple yet subtle style. I knew the methods by which, at will, he surrendered himself to joy or melancholy. I even tried to pilfer some of his secrets.

Then one day he disappeared, leaving no trace.

His friends notified the police and the detectives did their best, but in vain.

There was a suggestion that he had departed secretly to taste the pleasures of some tropical island and that the ship had been wrecked on the way.

But I think myself that he had voluntarily left a world, the enchantment of which he knew he had exhausted.

When I give my imagination full reign I see the poet, as though it were the most natural thing in the world, suddenly spread his wings and sail through the air to the enchanted lawns of the Elysian fields, bearing a crystal lute and picturesquely convoyed by a swarm of golden bees.

# The Crutches of Uncle Celestin

SHOULD a visitor to our house prove misguided enough to raise the subject of spiritualism, an expression of bored resignation would steal over the countenances of more than one member of the family. For we knew only too well that someone was certain to ask: "Do you know the story of our dear uncle Celestin and his crutches?"

If the guest had already heard it my brothers and sisters would rejoice, but should the reply be in the negative, they would relapse into gloom. The die was cast, they would feel. We have heard the tale of Uncle's crutches a hundred times and now we have got to listen to it all over again.

It is to put an end to this delusion of my family that I repeat the story today. Henceforth it will be sufficient to hand this book to those interested enough to read it.

My brothers and sisters are still ignorant of the key to the enigma and, if I have made up my mind to reveal it, it is in the hope that the truth may bring peace to a family that has suffered for so long under the persecution of its own members.

I have no clear recollection of Uncle Celestin. All I know is that he was small, completely bald, and very ugly.

But with this vague figure I do, on the other hand, associate a sound which beats on my memory, a toc-toc-toc which preceded and followed the appearance of the poor man. For Uncle Celestin was a cripple and walked only with the support of metal crutches, which had been patented by a German orthopedist, and the sound of the steel shafts on the floor advertised his coming and going.

He had always been lame, and the trouble, probably hip disease, becoming aggravated with age, my father had invited his brother (of whom he was not inordinately fond) to come and live under our roof. Our house in the country was of the bungalow type and thus saved the invalid the perpetual ascent and descent of the stairs that irked him in his town flat.

Uncle Celestin did not need persuading, and for more than ten years our whole house resounded to the intermittent tune of his steel crutches.

When he died nobody wept. He had exasperated us all to the last degree. His infirmity was not to blame; this alone would have endeared him to us, for we were not callous, but we suffered from its distressing consequences, as he could not forgive anyone among us for being normally built.

"Ah," he would say. "What's the good of having legs like yours if you are going to spend your days in the library?" or: "With legs like yours, falling off a horse is not mere clumsiness, it is pure imbecility!"

These comments were not really injurious. It was the frequency and regularity with which they were made that gave them something of the quality of the drops of water used by Chinese torturers: the progressive agony of an area that is perpetually attacked; the unendurable exasperation of the victim's nerves, ending in unconsciousness and followed by insanity.

Things were not so bad as all that and none of us died or became mad, but it is also lamentably true that, at the death of our uncle, our eyes remained dry, quite hopelessly dry.

As soon as the doctor had assured us that my uncle had really passed away my mother telephoned to the undertaker, the only one that existed in our little town, and asked him to make all arrangements for the funeral.

Evidently the undertaker had been on the watch for the unfortunate man's death, for less than an hour elapsed before the coffin was brought around.

It fitted him so exactly that the soles of his shoes and the skin of the shining crown of his bald head actually touched the two ends.

The undertaker seemed thoroughly pleased with this tribute to his precision.

It was then that he approached my mother and asked whether he should not also place in the coffin the crutches from which the poor invalid had never been separated during his lifetime.

## THE CRUTCHES OF UNCLE CELESTIN

My mother immediately agreed, but my father, on the contrary, declared, with a great deal of reason, that death had freed my uncle from all infirmity.

The coffin without crutches became a symbol of liberation, and my uncle's body was placed in it with nothing reminiscent of the misery of his life. After all, my father was Uncle Celestin's brother and his counsels prevailed, as they always did in our house.

The next day, that of the funeral, my father thought it proper to say farewell to his elder brother and, with a decisive gesture, threw back the pall with which the coffin had been draped, pending the screwing down of the lid.

He wished also to show the mortal remains of Uncle Celestin to those old friends who would not fail to pay him their last respects.

These came, it is true, but all refused to view the body, saying that they preferred to remember him as they last saw him, affable and smiling.

As a matter of fact I very much doubt whether they had ever seen him smile or could, at any time, have found him affable, but we have all, at some time or other, committed ourselves to such pious prevarications.

To return to my father. He had hardly lifted the pall before an exclamation of mingled surprise and annoyance escaped him.

For Uncle Celestin lay in his coffin, his lips stiff, his countenance austere, supported, as he had been in life, by his two crutches.

Very vexed at having been disobeyed, my father questioned in turn the servants, the undertaker's man, his wife, and his children, all of whom vigorously denied having touched the wretched crutches.

The irritation of the head of the family reached such a pitch that he interrogated them all, my brothers, sisters, the maids, and valets, once more, this time beside the coffin. I alone, of the entire household, was not questioned. I was six years old and was naturally spared that strange ceremony. It smacked of that medieval custom, by which suspected assassins were made to parade in front of the corpse of one who had died a violent death, on the assumption that the blood would flow from it should the author of the crime be present.

But on this occasion nothing of the sort happened, no one confessed to his guilt, and the affair remained shrouded in mystery. Had my uncle risen in the night to recover his crutches? My brothers and sisters did not say so, but they let it be understood by those who cared to believe it, and, more especially, by those who did not want to do so.

And, as I said in the beginning of this story, from then on no one could ever speak of phantoms or ghosts in our house without being automatically confronted with the irritating mystery of Uncle Celestin and his crutches.

I have promised to give the key to the enigma. Here it is.

My mother, my brothers, my sisters, the servants, in fact everyone had told the truth. None of them had touched the crutches of Uncle Celestin.

But I, too young, so they thought, to be cross-examined, I remember quite clearly unhooking them from the brass rail of the bed from which they were hanging.

I even remember the considerable effort it took to jam them, one after the other, up the very narrow space left between the already-rigid corpse of my uncle and his arms, into his armpits.

Small children have no prejudice against death, it would seem, and they do not fear it, or rather the dead.

In my eyes, it was simply Uncle Celestin who had gone to bed in his box.

And, as I realized that they were going to take him away, it seemed only proper that he should take with him those crutches with which he had surreptitiously administered many a blow to my posterior when he had surprised me playing on all fours on the Aubusson carpet of the drawing room, the carpet that, in my eyes, was such a marvelous garden. He would accompany the attack with a phrase that I can hear now.

"When people have such abominably fat limbs as yours, they don't drag themselves along the ground like a legless cripple!"

# Suspicion

It was in 1911. I was then sixteen years old and wanted one thing in the world: to go, alone, to the Great Brussels Exhibition.

Time and effort were needed to extract from my parents the required permission. They gave it at last, tired of the struggle, and one Friday (of evil omen!) I took the train to Basle, where I was to spend the night.

Elated by my new-found independence, I slipped into the last empty place in a second-class non-smoker. During the trip I looked feverishly at international time-tables and felt from time to time for the blue envelope near my heart which my father had given me, begging me not to waste its contents, and generally behaved in the best way to attract the attention of my fellow-travellers. And, oddly enough, that of a sharper . . . so that, when I reached Basle, the envelope and bank-notes had disappeared!

At once I complained to the station-master's office, where they seemed amused at my expense. Thoroughly crestfallen, I went off to spend the night with my godfather. The good man gave me a sum equal to the one I had lost, and was so kind, into the bargain, as to promise of his own accord to say nothing about my misfortunes, to spare me my father's wrath.

The next day I set off once more, but the scenery of Alsace and Luxembourg were of little interest. My companions of the previous day, their faces, their behaviour, haunted me, and besides, and most especially, the existence of my new fortune so carefully hidden in a waistcoat pocket. Of yesterday's nine fellow-travellers, which was the thief? Would he ever be discovered? And this time . . . should I be able to hold on to my possessions? Tormented by these questions and ferociously determined to protect myself from further theft, I began to take stock of the occupants of the carriage one by one. No doubt I looked disagreeable. I cannot otherwise explain the nervous attitude of an old lady who glanced at me, terrified, and seized the opportunity at our first stop to move into another coach. To all appearances, she was afraid of finding herself suddenly at close quarters with a dangerous individual, escaped from some asylum.

Little by little the carriage emptied, and two or three hours after we started, I was almost alone. Almost, but not quite; for one traveller remained . . . the one whose departure I could most vehemently have desired.

He was a sort of itinerant Hercules with short legs, short fingers, a huge head and powerful chest. The knife of a guillotine would hardly have found a place on his neck. Black hair, soaked in brilliantine and brushed down towards the eyebrows, narrowed still more an already low forehead. A week's growth on his face covered it nearly to the eyes, in which I had already noted a sharp glance and piercing look.

He was poorly dressed with studied bad taste, and I noticed the filthy collar and dirty nails. From these details and the olive tint of his skin I judged him to be from the Levant. He spoke to me once or twice, quite amiably, but I answered growling like an angry dog and he didn't insist.

I had foreseen what was going to happen. The fellow would worm his way into my confidence and was only waiting for a tunnel to empty my pockets. To my great surprise nothing happened at all. When I reached the station at Brussels, the bank-notes were still in their place inside my coat in a pocket carefully fastened with a safety-pin, which must have been oddly made because I pricked my fingers each time I tried to feel if my pocket-book was still there.

I got out first, very quickly and without looking behind me. It was dark. Clutching the handle of my suitcase tightly in my right hand, with the left on my chest, the dangerous side, I pushed my way through the crowd which filled the central hall and the underground passage. Just as I reached the exit, a vast shadow fell across the asphalt in a pool of electric light; my fellow-traveller had not left me. But he said nothing and I pretended not to have seen. Once on the pavement outside I hurried towards a near-by hotel. Then, ten paces farther on, animated by both fear

# SUSPICION

and curiosity, I turned my head. Motionless, still at the same spot, he was following me with his eyes. It was with great strides and beating heart that I reached the hotel . . . only to come out again almost at once. There was not a room to be had nor an empty bed, they said, and they advised me to try elsewhere. I was back on the pavement, searching the street round about with my eyes, but the man had disappeared.

Then began a series of wanderings that I still remember. Suitcase in hand, I went into all the neighboring hotels. All were full or offered for an impossible price a room with two beds and a bathroom. I called a cab and went clopping off to the part of the town nearer the centre, in search of hospitality. The answer was everywhere the same, and the cabman looked at me sarcastically, repeating every now and then: "Why didn't you reserve, Sir? In Brussels one reserves." I could have knocked him down!

Instead, I got out of his old trap and went on on foot, vainly searching. My suitcase seemed to increase in size and weight. Every five minutes I passed it from one hand to the other. Then, the height of bad luck, a fine rain began to fall and very soon soaked my clothes. Dripping, with my teeth chattering and trailing my suitcase, I looked shabby enough, and I attributed the invariable refusal of hotel-keepers less to their inability to put me up than to the fear of having to take me in for nothing. Just as I was repassing, with my head down, under the lights of a Palace Hotel which had been particularly unkind, a jolly voice hailed me and I turned round. It took me a few seconds to recognise the flashy individual I had left two hours before. He had shaved but he hardly looked much cleaner. "Ha, my young friend! Not a room free?"—"No, Sir," I said curtly. More and more jolly he went on: "That doesn't surprise me. I had to run North and South, East and West to find a bed!" I remember he said "Sowf," and this strange pronunciation increased my distrust. It seemed to me a part and parcel of his dishonest make-up. But he ran on more and more cordially: "Here they finally gave me a room with two beds. Take one of them. I should be so pleased!"

You can imagine, from what I have been saying, how delighted I was with this offer of hospitality! I had sufficient presence of mind to answer with increasing curtness: "You are very good, Sir, but I would rather look elsewhere."—"It's quite useless!" replied the huge fellow, who, obviously, was not easily put off . . . "You won't find even standing room, do you see? Not even a dog-kennel!" Then he put his hand on my shoulder . . . "Come on! Not so many compliments!"

Me, compliments indeed! Without leaving time to reply and tightening his hold on me affectionately, he called the porter: "Take this suitcase up to No. 117." Obviously my new friend was accustomed to big hotels and to being in command. Wet through as I was, what could I do but submit?

In the stranger's room I seemed to breathe an atmosphere uneasy and full of mystery. Quickly I changed my clothes and went to dine in a restaurant near-by. My first sight of the Exhibition would be a pleasure for the morrow. Besides, I felt in no mood for amusement. I was about to share the room of an individual who impressed me as being a brigand. My bed would be next to his. While I dined, these thoughts crowded my brain, and the luscious Belgian cooking tasted as insipid as chewed paper.

Sad at heart, I went back to the hotel. After wandering gloomily to and fro in the hall to kill time, I returned still more gloomily to No. 117. There a pleasant surprise awaited me. My room-mate was not yet back. His absence would make it possible to hide the pocket-book under the sheets. It would have been so easy to deposit it at the office! But at sixteen one can't think of everything. And I had become so suspicious. So far as honesty went, I only believed in my own! In a second I was undressed and had slipped into bed. Lying on my side, my face to the wall, I could feel distinctly between my ribs and my hip a small lump . . . the pocket-book.

Then I began to wait: to wait for the terrible, the inevitable to happen. I thought I heard a stealthy tread. I thought I felt a hand slide down among the sheets. Every now and then I raised myself on my pillow, but only to find that I was the victim of my own imagination and absolutely alone in "our" room. In the end, the emotion and fatigue were too strong for me. In spite of my effort of will and the light which I had on purpose omitted to put out, I fell into a dreamless sleep.

Suddenly I opened my eyes. In the darkness some one had seized me by the shoulder. The man was there, standing by my bed, bending over me. My bed was no longer a bed but a lift falling down from the sixth

# SUSPICION

floor. I wanted to speak; my voice choked in my throat. How could I get to the electric bell? Could I struggle with this Hercules? Could I scream?

"Well, young man," said a cordial voice, "you seem to have had a good night, eh?" At that moment I felt like a man who is going to be smashed to death on the pavement and who suddenly finds himself sitting in an arm-chair without knowing how he came there. "If I wake you," went on the voice, "it is because I want to ask you to do me a service."

The shutters, pushed by vigorous hand, flew open and the room was bathed in light. "I have something to do in town," continued my companion, coming back to me. "You would oblige me enormously by taking care of this little bag for half-an-hour." Dumbfounded, with blinking eyes, I had just enough presence of mind to stammer a few polite words and hold out my hand. My companion put a little bag into it, smiled and nodded, and was gone.

I looked at the coarse linen bag, tied with a simple string but very solidly made. It went in to join my pocket-book. The Brussels sun seemed to have risen for me alone. I dressed without haste this time and breakfasted with a fine appetite, my mind delivered of its nightmare. Today I still remember with pleasure the cup of coffee and the *cranik*, a sort of currant bun, essentially Flemish, that one can never forget. Just as I was finishing, a step easy to recognise was heard down the corridor. In advance, to prevent any looking into the depths of my coat, I took out the bag. Just as well to be careful to the end!

My Levantine seemed to be in a most excellent temper. As a man of education, he began by saying thank you. Then, to my great surprise, he undid the string and spread out the contents of the little sack on the table. Completely dazzled, my eyes opened and shut. A hundred brilliants sparkled on the red cloth. "I am a diamond merchant," explained the big man, "and, by Jove, I don't care to walk about with a fortune like that in my pocket. But when I saw you get into that railway carriage yesterday, I knew at once one could trust you with anything!"

A quarter of an hour later we separated with a handshake and I never saw my diamond merchant again.

# At the Spanish Customhouse

*I* ONCE HAD AN adventure when traveling," said my father. "An experience which might have ended badly and which was connected with a precious stone. That sort of thing seems to be becoming a tradition with us."

I was very anxious to hear more. It would not be unpleasant to find, between my father and myself, a sort of parity in misfortune. When I pressed him to tell me the story he did not need much persuasion. It is now twenty years old, but I give it here as faithfully as my memory permits.

"About ten years ago," he said, "family affairs took me to Spain where one of my cousins was getting married. My luggage was strapped and I was about to leave when a friend that I had not seen since I left college was announced. From vague rumors I had gathered that he lived in the Spanish colonies and had business interests there.

" 'Say that I am leaving in a few minutes for abroad and that I cannot see anyone,' I said.

"The servant returned almost immediately to say that the visitor insisted on seeing me. He had just learned that I was going to Madrid and it was precisely on that account that he was anxious to speak to me.

"My curiosity aroused, I gave in, and into my office was shown a big-bellied, exuberant, breathless, rather congested individual, his neck compressed into a distressingly brightly colored collar. His whole aspect had become rather vulgar and I had difficulty in recognizing him.

"He must have found me changed, judging from his expression on seeing me, an expression which he was quick to cover with a rather unconvincing smile. He hurried toward me, his hands extended.

" 'My old friend! Quite unchanged! But this is no time for compliments, much as we deserve them. I do not want to risk making you lose your train. Here is the crux of the matter. I may as well say at once that I have come to ask you to do me a small service.'

"Long experience had taught me what these little services may cost, and I am afraid he could have derived no encouragement from my face. I was going to be 'touched' again, and I cursed myself for my own weakness in allowing this jackanapes inside the house.

"But I did my friend Ernest an injustice. He pulled a little box out of his pocket and handed it to me.

" 'Would it trouble you too much to take this enormous trunk to Madrid? Someone will take it off your hands either at the hotel or at your cousin's.'

"The request seemed harmless enough, and I could not refuse it without seeming disobliging. But as an act of precaution I was determined to know more.

" 'What is in it?'

"Ernest opened the box and produced what looked like a dirty and irregularly shaped lump of sugar.

" 'What is it?'

"Ernest chuckled.

" 'A precious stone. An uncut diamond and, as you may have observed, a pretty big one.'

" 'Good Lord!' I exclaimed. 'You ought to have remembered that in the old days I was appallingly absent-minded! And I have not improved with age. Supposing I was to drop that lump of sugar in my cup of coffee?'

" 'There is no need to exaggerate,' remarked Ernest placidly. 'You would find the pebble again at the bottom of your cup and would have rendered me a service for which I shall be most grateful.'

"Curiosity impelled me to a fourth question.

" 'And . . . might I ask for whom . . . ?'

"An indefinable expression, in which I thought I detected more than a touch of malice, passed over Ernest's face.

" 'Oh, that,' he said lightly, 'is of no importance.'

"It was impossible to press him further or to hesitate any longer. I placed the box in the securest pocket of my waistcoat. I reflected that if my friend Ernest was still acting up to his reputation as a lady-killer it was small wonder that the diamond was so large.

"I parted with him without regret and shortly afterward boarded the train. The express rattled along at fifty miles an hour, which in those days was a maximum speed, and those travelers who braved it were perhaps justified in considering themselves fairly courageous; but I was not concerned with collisions or derailments. My mind, like yours, was on other things.

"In the pocket of my waistcoat I was carrying a diamond worth a fortune and I was responsible for it.

"As the train traveled on toward Spain I eyed my fellow passengers with suspicion, and from time to time explored my pocket with my fingers. Then, suddenly, a very natural sequence of ideas induced a new preoccupation. How had Ernest acquired this diamond and why this reticence when I asked him about its destination?

"One after another old memories began to assail me. In his college days Ernest had not shown himself too scrupulous. What guarantee had I of his honesty now? In entrusting me with this stone had he meant to use me as an intermediary in some shady deal?

"If this were so I might very well find myself involved in something unsavory. I had reached this point when an appalling thought struck me. Where had my wits been?

"The customhouse! I had suddenly remembered that twin sister of the exchequer, all the more formidable because the law protects the safe of the taxpayer and remains silent on the subject of fraudulent returns, but it gives the customhouse officer the right to open the trunks and examine the pockets of the traveler, and the moment it suspects a lie it exposes it to broad daylight.

"Should I declare the stone? To that question both my conscience and the law replied in unison: 'Yes.' But to that 'yes' a third influence, pitiless or complaisant, according to circumstance, raised some very practical objections.

"Supposing I declared it and discovered that my suspicions were well founded? Then there was the duty. It would certainly be heavy, and I was carrying only enough money for my journey and visit to Madrid.

On the other hand, by defrauding the customs I should become liable to a fine which would probably be enormous!

"What a fool I had been! Never again would I indulge in sentimentality over old college friends! I would give anything now to know Ernest's address though I had congratulated myself at the time on my prudence in not asking for it. No, nothing would induce me to declare it! The time for recrimination was over, and the only thing to do now was to put a good face on things.

"But what sort of face?

"On reflection it seemed to me best to adopt a carefree attitude and pretend to be half asleep. It was thus that I approached the customs officer to whom I announced, between yawns, that I had nothing to declare. The official evidently thought that so sleepy a traveler must, of necessity, be innocent, for he threw a mere glance at my suitcase and passed me through. I got back into my carriage and the train started at once. With a sigh of relief I settled comfortably down to sleep.

"I was rudely disturbed by a whistle. The train stopped. Hardly a minute had passed since our departure. What was happening?

"I opened the window. A hundred yards away I could see the red lights of the customs and they seemed to me hateful, glaring like a reproach against the dark background of the sky.

"Steps approached and the sound of voices. They were looking for someone, calling out a name that was disconcertingly familiar.

"The sounds became more distinct. It was my own name that was echoing so untiringly in the night. This time I should have to pay for my audacity. I put my head out of the window.

" 'Here,' I cried peevishly. 'What is it? What do you want?'

"An official ran along the track, drew himself up with military precision, clicked his heels, and requested me to follow him to the customs office. Meanwhile, the train waited, the heads of my fellow travelers, hanging as though guillotined out of windows, staring at me with hostile curiosity.

"I was taken to the office. The customs official was seated at one end of the room, separated both from his staff and the importunate by a green carpet. Two superb and herculean gendarmes, the expression of whose black eyes filled me with foreboding, hemmed me in on either side. My

# AT THE SPANISH CUSTOMHOUSE

apprehensions were not allayed by the interrogation which took place after my papers had been examined.

" 'You are the owner of this passport?'

" 'Yes, Captain.'

" 'From Basle, Switzerland?'

" 'Exactly.'

" 'Going to Madrid?'

" 'That is right.'

" 'Well, señor, a few minutes ago at the customs you declared that you had nothing to declare.'

"My wits had not completely deserted me. I answered with a certain cunning.

" 'To declare? What should I have declared?'

" 'The diamond, señor, the diamond.'

"Who could have betrayed me? That pest Ernest. And if so, with what end in view?

" 'You are carrying a diamond, is that not so?'

"Now was the moment of all others to keep calm.

" 'A diamond? Certainly,' I replied.

"From my tone I might have been speaking of an umbrella.

"The official gave an exclamation of relief.

" 'You have given us a good fright, monsieur,' he said. 'The Central Bureau of Police in Madrid informed us that a Swiss gentleman, whose name and description they furnished, was about to pass through our customs, and that he was the bearer of a diamond intended for our Queen! And you did not declare it or make yourself known. We believed you to have been kidnaped or assassinated and I took upon myself to have the train stopped to make sure of your presence, with a view to instituting an inquiry should that prove necessary.'

"I was in Spain, the home of chivalry and the holder of great traditions. My answer was that of a hidalgo.

" 'I did not know that you had been informed. The diamond was intended for a woman and a queen, so I held my tongue. I am ready to pay the fine.'

"The official rose to his feet.

" 'Go back to your train, monsieur. I only regret that I have made our gracious sovereign wait even for a minute. And do not be nervous. Two policemen in plain clothes have instructions to take care of you.'

"He accompanied me to the door and, at parting, pressed my hand.

" '*Vaya con Dios*,' he said."

# Friends

*I* spent that summer in a charming inn near Dives. It was called the Hôtel de la Reine Jeanne. From the doorway one was struck by the cheerful note of the copper pots that seemed to illuminate a kitchen that gave on to the yard. In the depths of this kitchen a Norman cook, with bare arms and a white cap, might be seen standing near an old-fashioned stove, tossing pancakes in a brass pan.

The summer months were cloudless and I do not remember one drop of rain. But I have not forgotten the thirsts of those months of July and August, the foaming glasses of cider, my solitary table under a plane tree on a lawn gay with zinnias, the striped umbrellas, dotted at random over the grass like gigantic flowers that had sprung from the earth in response to the wand of a magic gardener.

But when I try to remember my room I find that I have forgotten everything about it but the window, which looked onto the axis of a narrow street over which seven centuries had passed—a street that opened onto the sea and whose medieval architecture, a church and cloister, a spire erect as a taper, an arch bowed like a bent spine, Christian symbols of penitence and prayer, framed in the waves that had brought the pagans from the north to conquer Normandy.

Everything about the hotel of the Reine Jeanne pleased me, both the present and the memories of ancient days. And yet there was a sadness about the place, a sadness that penetrated even into the houses. The streets were silent. I was the only guest in the hotel with the exception of occasional birds of passage on Sundays. But the cook did not fail to prepare menus for the solitary guest that would satisfy the most fastidious palate.

Installed under the branches of my plane tree I did them justice. But, between mouthfuls, I listened to a sound coming from beyond the horizon, an incessant rumbling not unlike the noise of the surf, less regular, more confused, but, at times, as rhythmic as the sea. Today, as I recall it, I would compare it with the alternately too slow and too fast beat of a diseased heart. It was in 1916, and a furious battle was raging on the frontier of Flanders. That noise was the sound of guns. An echo of frightfulness, it penetrated to that peaceful corner of Normandy. And even when it failed to reach us the mere aspect of the village spoke of war.

Women had replaced the men. In passing down the streets one could see a woman at the butcher's stall and in the chemist's dispensary. As drummers they transmitted to the population the municipal orders; as postmen they trudged along the white roads in the midday heat, blinded with sun and dust.

A few men remained, but one did not often see them. They hid, as though for shame that they, too, were not part of that monstrous heart whose beat was in our ears. Those that did not hide were old men or children who were too young to kill—yet.

The old men now scythed the grain, taking up once more the tool that they had not handled for twenty years. They progressed with short steps, and their diminished gestures did not extend very far now with the sweep of the blade. At the end of five minutes the worker would stop, pant for a time, and then return to his task. And this would go on for a long time.

The teams once harnessed, children would drive them. Without realizing it they had acquired the expressions and gestures of grown men.

There was not a fisherman on the jetty; they were all down there at the front. The old men were not strong enough for the work and the children were not allowed to go out with the boats which constituted the only capital of the families. The port was full of idle boats, floating side by side on the water like empty coffins.

Early one morning I leaned out of the window and was surprised by an unaccustomed spectacle. A boat was putting out to sea. Getting hastily into a linen suit and espadrilles, I went out to see what was happening.

There were three boys in the boat. All three exhibited the thin faces of children who have grown too fast, and all three had the same tousled

# FRIENDS

mops of hemp-colored hair. Barefooted, their emaciated bodies swathed in their fathers' cast-off blue woolen jerseys, with trousers of blue ticking or brown wool secured around the waist with tarred rope, they were trying to launch the boat in imitation of their elders. And they were making an uncommonly good job of it.

The eldest, a growing lad whose brown eyes, flecked with gold, seemed almost swamped in a myriad of freckles, was in command and gave his orders, punctuating them with oaths, the pungency of which would have satisfied an old shellback.

One could deal with this future seawolf. I approached him.

"I am very fond of fishing," I said, "and if I shall not be in the way I should like to go with you."

He examined me from top to toe, seemed perplexed, scratched his head, spat into the sea, and, at last, announced that he could not take me on board.

"There is no wind, you see. We shall probably have to row, in which case weight counts."

During that inspection I had been assessed at so many kilos, like a barrel of herrings, and discarded as too heavy, but I refused to admit defeat.

"I will row as much as you like," I said.

"You know how to row, you?"

"I am used to rowing, sailing, and fishing. I have passed my life on the water."

I prudently omitted to add that the water was that of the Swiss lakes.

The captain of the vessel hesitated for a moment, and then abruptly made up his mind.

"All right. You'll do," he said condescendingly. "You can come aboard."

I embarked. Before long the attitude of the skipper became less grim. Apparently I was not proving too unhandy. There was a light breeze, and a single sheet was sufficient to carry us to the open sea. Once there the boys began to cast the net, using only such words as were necessary. I can still see the color of the waves and smell the sea. I can remember the slow hauling in of the nets, heavy with fish, and the wet splash that ensued as they emptied themselves of their burden into a scattered moving heap of burnished silver that piled ever higher in the bottom of the boat, and the faces of my companions, for a day like this was a windfall and the three boys were beaming. With winks and smiles they made me party to their adventure, and I responded as best I could without fully understanding their meaning.

When the time came to return I looked at my watch. It was two o'clock in the afternoon. The breeze had veered and become a stiff wind blowing from the shore, which boded ill for our journey home. It was impossible to sail free and our only chance was to tack.

At the end of an hour we were near the land, but still a long way from the port. The tide had begun to ebb, and the combined wind and current were carrying us out to sea. Our only chance was to reef and row against the tide toward the cliffs outlined against the skyline.

I do not think I have ever taken so much exercise and trust that I shall never be called upon to work so hard again. For four hours we had struggled, those three children and I, against the force that was driving us seaward. It was nearly six when we reached port, and we were exhausted. As I stepped ashore I glanced at my companions. The two youngest were white under their tan.

It was a comfort to feel the ground under one, but when I let go of the oars the skin of my hands remained behind. Yet another illusion went up in smoke! I had thought myself so thoroughly hardened by long days spent in rowing on the Swiss lakes!

We bade each other a cordial good-by and I tottered toward the inn. I had not gone far before I heard a hail. I turned. Georges Parent, the skipper, using his two hands as a megaphone, wanted to know my address. Till then he had not impressed me as a sociable being and I was surprised at his question. Using the same method, I gave him the information he required and hurried on my way, impatient to dress my blistered hands and get between the sheets.

Long before my usual time I was awakened next morning. Someone was knocking at my door.

"Come in," I called, with justifiable irritation.

The door opened to admit the chambermaid. She was tousled and obviously had dressed in a hurry. She also seemed both sleepy and bad-tempered.

"Monsieur," she announced, in a voice that justified my suspicions, "there is a man downstairs who wants to speak to you."

There was a possibility that my brother might have found himself in this neighborhood and called on me, but I had gone away without leaving any address, and this unexpected visit was surprising.

"Tell the gentleman to come up," I said.

"It is not a gentleman, it is a man," retorted the chambermaid, without moving.

"Very well then, I will come down."

A thought struck me. It was probably one of my cronies of yesterday who had been deputed by the others to call on me. Probably their appetites had been roused by the success of the night before, and he had come to ask for further assistance.

"He has chosen a good moment," I thought, glancing at my hands, the palms of which looked like slices of bread and jam.

I was right. In the yard, his back against the trunk of a plane tree, stood Georges Parent. When he saw me he snatched off his beret and walked with a true seaman's roll toward me. He stood twisting his cap in his hands. When he spoke it was with difficulty.

"Good morning, monsieur," he said, still maltreating his beret.

"Good morning, my friend, what wind blows you here?"

"It's like this, monsieur. There's something I want to say to you. Last night we went to Villers . . ."

He stopped, fumbling for words.

"To Villers?" I said encouragingly. "After a day like that? Was not the afternoon backbreaking enough?"

"Yes—that is to say—no. Anyway, we sold our fish at Villers, thirteen kilos of fish at nine francs the kilo."

"For your sake I am very glad to hear it," I exclaimed sincerely.

"That makes one hundred and seventeen francs," calculated Georges Parent.

What was he driving at?

"Well, it's like this. Anyway, we thought you'd worked as much, even more than us. So I've brought you your share."

Without waiting for an answer he fumbled in his pocket, then thrust his upturned hand toward me in that gesture that serves alike for the giving and receiving of alms.

"That makes six *écus*," he said.

It is difficult to put my feelings into words. I think perhaps that now, for the first time, I knew the true meaning of the word "tenderness."

"Keep the money," I said, with a catch in my throat. "I could not dream of taking it."

A dark flush spread over his freckled face and his eyes hardened.

"Isn't it enough? Why won't you take it?"

I realized that I had hurt him and hastened to repair my blunder.

"I expressed myself badly, Georges," I said, calling him for the first time by his Christian name. "I went with you because I liked it, because I enjoy fishing and rowing."

"Yes," agreed Georges, suddenly mollified. "But when you came you did not know that you would have to row for four hours or more. That there would be the tide and the wind and that you would get wet."

Without more ado he thrust the six écus into my hand.

"Then I accept it with thanks," I said. "But on one condition. That all three of you dine with me tonight at the restaurant of the Poule d'Or."

He needed no persuasion. He accepted and rolled off, smiling once more.

My guests arrived on the stroke. They had made a careful toilet, that is to say, they had brushed their clothes and plastered their unruly hair with water.

It was very cheerful, that first and last meal I took in the company of my three fishermen. We drank cider and burgundy and our tongues were loosened. We consumed a leg of mutton and left nothing but a bone decorated with parsley. And we separated at last with a handclasp and an "*au revoir*."

Next day I left Dives and the sea. It seemed that the little sailors had gone out of my life, but at Christmas I received a card signed by Georges Parent.

"Come and fish with us in the spring," he wrote, "as soon as it gets warmer. You will bring us luck."

I answered cordially but without committing myself, and that year my steps did not take me back to Dives.

Next year brought another card. It was sent from Champagne.

"It is very cruel here," it said simply, "and every day I miss the sea."

I posted one of those nondescript packages to him that delight soldiers at the front. I had no answer.

A year after the war had ended I motored through Dives. I could see the Hôtel de la Reine Jeanne in the distance, but I lacked the courage to stop and examine the names on the War Memorial.

# Souvenir of Hammam Meskoutine

**O**N MY FIRST ENTRANCE into the white, blue, and gilt bedroom I looked with a smile of satisfaction at the freshly distempered walls, the sky-blue cambric muslin curtains, the cedarwood fire that burned with an odor of incense in the grate, and at the shining copper bars of the English double bed in which I was joyously preparing to sleep alone. I was to be disappointed. But I hasten to add that my experience had no "next morning." On the contrary, the days followed each other, and I reposed peacefully in the comfortable bed, blessing the waters of a spring that restored me to second youth and to which I shall not fail to return to capture a third, should I feel the need.

My room was as gay as one could desire. The french window opened onto a terrace, below which was a charming inner court, planted with high palms, bedecked with bougainvillia and dignified by Roman statues, the result of various excavations. Their heads, legs, and arms proved that these springs had been well known to the conquerors of Carthage.

On the first night I had gone to bed in an excellent humor. And yet ...

I woke about one o'clock in the morning. There was someone in my room, quite close to my bed. There could be no possible doubt about it. I could hear the sound of uneven breathing so distinctly that it could not possibly come from the next room.

I stretched out a hand in the darkness and felt for the electric switch, in vain. I could not find it.

But I did find, by groping, a bedside table, and on it a candle and a box of matches. I was astonished at this discovery, as I had no recollection of the existence of any such thing.

I lighted the candle and looked around me, utterly bewildered.

I no longer found myself in the magnificent double bed, but in a narrow iron one, half a bed one might almost call it.

And the room seemed to have been stripped. The window curtains had disappeared, there was no longer any sign of electric fittings on the walls. But, by way of compensation, by the side of my bed I could distinguish another exactly like it. It was occupied by "the thing" whose halting respiration had awakened me!

I say "the thing" because, at first sight, I could not tell its nature.

It was, so it seemed to me, a human being, wrapped from head to foot in bandages of fine gauze, looking like nothing so much as a mummy bound in linen wrappings.

Its chest rose and fell spasmodically, and, in so doing, gave out the whistling, or, rather, groaning noise that had awakened me.

This head without a face was alarming to look at and produced in me a phenomenon well known to all who dream a great deal—a curious sensation of diminution. I realized that I was not awake.

"What an abominable dream!" I thought, and, to escape from the unpleasant sight of this swaddled figure, I turned my head and stared at the wall, only to recoil with a shudder of disgust.

For the distemper was bespattered with blood. And it had flowed in sufficient abundance to form rivulets which ran, half coagulated, the whole length of the wall, meandering right up to my bed.

I was then conscious of such a violent loathing, such a vivid impression of horror, that I woke, my hands like ice, my forehead damp with sweat.

This time I had no trouble in finding the switch, and the room was flooded suddenly with electric light, that light so motionless and implacable, so fitted to exorcise ghosts. I found myself back in the spruce bedroom, in the spacious bed in which I had gone to sleep that night.

All that I have described here would be devoid of interest if it dealt with an ordinary nightmare. But next day I told my dream to one of the habitués of the watering place and beheld a man stupefied with astonishment.

"What I am going to tell you is simply amazing," he said. "For years now I have been in the habit of leaving Algiers every spring to take the cure in this charming place. I came here during the war. At that time there were several military doctors here who attributed to these waters

# SOUVENIR OF HAMMAM MESKOUTINE

certain healing qualities in the case of wounds. To test their theory they chose for experiment soldiers who had been terribly burnt by the petrol from *Flammen-werfer*. Two of these unfortunate men occupied the very room in which you are sleeping. They were, if I remember rightly, lying side by side, in two little iron beds, completely swathed in gauze bandages soaked in olive oil and mineral water. Your description of the room, just as it was at the time, and of its wretched inhabitants, is, with the exception of one detail, absolutely exact. The markings you saw on the wall certainly existed! But there was no question of blood! Like most of their comrades, the two Legionnaires were inveterate chewers of tobacco, and with the simplicity of all heroes they ejected the juice of their favorite weed against the walls, hence the graffiti that you saw. A good deal of trouble was taken to hide them under the fresh plaster!"

I hold here, between my hands, a fine vulcanite disk which I am examining with curiosity.

A chemist, if he were to analyze it, would see in it simply two hundred grams of resinous and sulphurous matter.

It is a gramaphone record and it enshrines "The Death of Otello," sung by Tamagno, the great nineteenth-century tenor, dead thirty years ago. One has merely to place it on the machine, that is to say, to put it in contact with a certain number of essential physical elements, to revive all the genius, the personality, the actual performance of the singer who is no longer with us. And if a few grams of resinous matter, a few ounces of sulphur, are enough to produce this miracle, is it so absurd to believe that a room, walls and furniture, might, to a certain extent, absorb the waves of suffering that manifested themselves there during weeks, even months? Is it absurd to suggest that they might, under certain conditions, reproduce this terrible deposit?

But I promised, in my preface, not to try to explain the inexplicable.
And a promise should be kept.

# The Hairy Hand

In the month of May 1926 I was on board my boat and had sighted Malacca, when a heat wave spread over the Straits and caused the thermometer, which already stood at ninety-three in the shade, to mount by nine degrees.

These conditions endured for several days, until I believe I was at my last gasp. It was not, properly speaking, that I was ill. Heat has always affected me rather after the manner of an agreeable narcotic, but when I looked in the glass it reflected the image of something little better than a specter.

I recognized the malady and its source. It was necessary to find a remedy, and there was only one: to run away from the heat wave.

Flee? But where to? To Europe? To reach Europe one had to get across the Red Sea and, at that time of year, the Red Sea was a sea of molten metal. Fifteen days of this crossing and the *Pilsna* would have deposited yet another mummy on the wharf at Marseilles!

China was a long way off. I could find only one reasonable solution, and I adopted it without hesitation.

Avoiding Calcutta, I must put in at Georgetown. I could then spend the time necessary for my recovery on the island of Penang. The climate in the plains is tropical, but a funicular would take me to the altitude of cool nights and tepid mornings.

Two days later I was established a thousand meters above the sea in the only hotel in the neighborhood, a one-storied building covered with a flat roof and surrounded by a garden, a grass plot flaming with hibiscus.

As the thermometer registered a fall of ten degrees centigrade, so, slowly but surely, sleep and appetite returned to me, and my curiosity as well as my health reacted to this change of itinerary. For the first time I found myself in a hotel where everyone—staff, management, and guests—were, with the exception of myself, Chinese.

The cooking also was Chinese and I felt no desire to complain of it. With this ancient people, of a race that was already civilized at a time when many Europeans were still gnawing chunks of bison on the thresholds of their smoky caves, the art of the palate is based on a great principle which I have always admired. Among the dishes provided by the cooks of the Celestial Empire there is nothing that is not eatable. One can, with complete confidence, enjoy stoneless cherries and chicken and fish without bones.

My surroundings, on the other hand, inspired me at first with a certain distrust which I soon discovered was reciprocated. The men, smooth-faced, severely helmeted in white, wearing European clothing of white linen, watched me unceasingly. The women, with their high crowns of black plaits, all of them dressed in black or puce-colored silk embroidered in bright colors, the tunic blouse with its stiff, high collar reaching to the ears; wide, ankle-length trousers, sandals, and white cotton stockings, their feet divided in half like the hoof of an ox, all of them scented with ylang-ylang, and all alike (at the end of three weeks I was still unable to distinguish a single one of them), seemed to ignore me so long as I was in their presence.

But the moment I turned my back they broke into whispers the sibilance of which reached me from afar and pursued me with the insistence of a fly.

Men and women, they almost all of them knew English, but between themselves and at meals they spoke Chinese. And it added not a little to my discomfort to hear, without understanding, this language of soft vowels and sharp consonants, devoid of inflections or sonority, invertebrate and cruel.

The surroundings also were bizarre. Not far from the place where I was staying stood a building well known to tourists, the Temple of Serpents. Here venomous reptiles, the color of jade, were worshiped. They glided along the vermilion lacquered walls, insinuated themselves into the hollows of the volutes, and, intertwined, overflowed the sacred

# THE HAIRY HAND

vases. Several of the inhabitants of the hotel frequented the Temple regularly. They went there to make their devotions and offer a tribute of fresh eggs to the undulating divinities of the place, and this practice roused in me certain suspicions. At night, on returning to my room, I was quite prepared to discover, lurking under my pillow, a snake strayed from the sacred enclosure and more or less innocently transported in the folds of a wide silken sleeve.

In spite of this my stay at Penang was not unenjoyable. All told, these oddities provided me with more diversion than discomfort, and at the end of three weeks I found little pleasure in preparing to leave the hotel, though I had been living in a state of complete isolation. On the eve of my departure, after lunch and for the first time, I addressed a few words to the young woman who sat at her husband's side facing me and whom I had never seen raise the eyes she kept obstinately fixed on her plate. I had picked up her handkerchief, a hemstitched square of white linen, that had slipped to the ground as she was leaving the table. She thanked me adequately, with indifference, in two English monosyllables, during which her husband watched me out of the corners of his slanting eyes.

That night we dined at the usual time in the general dining room. Under the petrol lamps which dispensed a parsimonious light deadened still further by shades of waxed linen, I consumed the floury cream of a *beignet de soya*, flavored with syrup of litchis, to the accompaniment of the gentle clacking of the chopsticks of the Chinese guests. Then, suddenly, I received a shock. On the cloth, at the corner of the table, a finger appeared, a hairy finger, a human finger. Almost at once a second finger materialized and hooked itself onto the edge of the table, next door to the first.

The middle and third fingers appeared next. Only the thumb remained hidden. Then, suddenly, the four fingers disappeared.

I had recovered my composure. No doubt some domestic, crouching on the floor and hidden by the hanging folds of the tablecloth, was picking up stray scraps. However, as this invisible companionship did not appeal to me, I pushed back my chair, and bending forward lifted the cloth with a sweep of my hand. The space between the legs of the table was empty.

As I raised myself, dumfounded, I encountered the gaze of the Chinese sitting opposite. Over his face, inscrutable as that of an idol, slipped a smile, the sly smile of the yellow man. His wife, impassive, continued to eat, her eyes fixed on her plate. Apparently she had seen nothing.

Was it a hallucination? Had I been poisoned by some oriental drug?

The question had hardly crossed my mind when the finger reappeared, hesitatingly. Then another. Then all the others. And finally, with no arm to follow it, I saw coming in my direction a hand, cut off, sombre and hairy.

In a second I was on my feet.

It is here, that hand, fastened to a cork base, in a glass frame. I look at it sometimes with complaisance. And underneath that full-sized mummified hand may be read the words I wrote there:

*Mygale Spider*
*Specimen captured at Penang, May 28, 1926*
*The bite is dangerous. Sometimes fatal.*

The day after my return to Europe I received an envelope with a Malacca stamp. It contained a little white handkerchief which I recognized.

> # Accessory

WHEN my father declared that there was some uncanny link between our family and precious stones he was not far wrong. For the second time the possession of a stone was to involve me in an adventure which, on this occasion, came near to ending badly.

It began with an expedition by canoe along the Kulu-Ganga, a river that hides treasures in its alluvium. There is a place where Malay and Cingalese boys, hidden behind enclosures, drag these riches from the mud in which they are buried, and I had promised myself the pleasure of seeing these stones fished up like oysters, their fire scintillating between slime-daubed fingers.

But my disillusionment was complete. On that day I realized the truth of the adage I had learned at school: "When precious stones are in the rough they resemble broken bottle glass, minus the reflections." Disappointed, I went back to the canoe to resume my butterfly hunt farther up near the source of the river. Under the strokes of the paddle the boat glided, beneath a brazen sky, between clusters of pink nenuphars. Enormous bamboos grew on either bank, their crests meeting across the river and their leaves intermingling, so that alternate zones of light and shade stretched across the water. There was no sound in the forest, neither the cry of a beast nor the song of a bird. Every now and then a swift shadow would pass over the boat, and, lifting my head, I would see the two wings of a flying fox, reddish stains on the luminous background of the sky. Between that alternating light and shadow I felt overcome by torpor. I might have dropped off to sleep, lost my paddle, and allowed the canoe to drift if I had not been roused by the sound of splashing behind. I swung round. Was the boat being pursued? If so, was it by man or beast?

A man was swimming after me. He was young, quite naked, and molded like a bronze statue. With each stroke his finely modeled head, crowned with black hair that was kept severely in place by a cord knotted at the back of his neck, rose above the water. He was trying to join me, and, feeling rather puzzled, I stopped.

In a few seconds he had reached the stern. He gripped it with his hands and spat. A light like the wing of a kingfisher flashed over the side of the boat and was extinguished with a dry "plop."

"Great sapphire," jabbered the Hindu in bad English. "Very big, very fine. What give?"

My journeys in far countries had made me suspicious. I was familiar with Egypt and the sellers of false scarabs who swarm around the pyramids. Was this seller of precious stones offering me a bit of paste?

I picked up the stone and turned it in every direction under the level rays of the sun. Six branches of silver appeared, in turn, in its blue depths, like the rays of the moon on a summer night. It was the hexagonal star which, in certain sapphires, marks the axis of crystallization and which no maker of false stones has ever been able to reproduce. It was real! And how beautiful it was.

I felt in my pockets. I had three hundred rupees, about twelve hundred francs of Swiss money.

"Will you take these three hundred rupees?"

He shook his head. I had expected as much, and the sapphire was returned to its owner, who put it in his mouth and swam away.

I picked up my paddle, but I had gone only a few strokes when I was hailed once more. The Hindu had returned and was hanging with one hand onto the stern of the canoe. With his free hand he was offering me something.

"Master," he said faintly, "give the money and take the stone."

He seemed exhausted and I was suddenly moved to pity.

"Do you want to come aboard?" I asked, pointing to the canoe.

He made a fleeting gesture in the negative. After a moment, during which his eyes raked the bank, he pointed with his finger to a place where the forest became denser.

# ACCESSORY

"There," he said.

I paddled obediently in the direction he had indicated. As soon as the Hindu touched bottom he stopped me. Up to his belt in water, looking like some river god of the old fables, he pulled at the locks of hair clinging to his forehead until he had puffed them up into a kind of nest. Then he increased the tension of the cord by tightening the knot at the back of his neck and held out his hand.

"First, notes."

I gave him the notes. He counted them, then rolled them one after another in his fingers. When he had reduced them to small compact cylinders like cigarettes, he slipped them one by one into the cavity in his hair. This done, he held out his hand for the second time. Some pieces of silver and small change fell into it.

Then the surprising thing happened. He changed color. From his girdle to his hair, all that I could see of his skin became cinder gray. A week passed in the Indies is enough to teach a foreigner what this means. The man was afraid.

He closed his hand on his booty, and in a few seconds he had covered the space that separated him from the bank, slipped between the trunks of the bamboos, and disappeared.

And I became very thoughtful. Was this a case of a stolen jewel?

I had not concluded a bargain such as this without scruples, having obviously acquired a stone for much less than it was worth, but, in the end, any remorse I may have felt evaporated. This sapphire merchant would certainly have found a less scrupulous collector than myself and the find might have disappeared, as so many other treasures have done, into the coffers of some maharajah. And perhaps this one was worth less than I had thought. I searched the newspapers carefully every night and was reassured. There was no mention of any theft in them.

A month later I found myself in that half-European, half-Cingalese town, Colombo, in the streets of which luxurious shops and the most primitive stalls elbow each other. In the course of a stroll I came on a jeweler in whose window unset precious stones were artfully displayed in velvet trays, cleverly arranged according to color. Over the door was a Dutch name, very well known in Ceylon.

I went in. A stout, fair gentleman came to meet me. He had that unostentatious air of authority that one sees in superior officers, cabinet ministers, priests, and those big dealers who specialize in objects de luxe that appeal to women, in fact in all those whose business controls the world.

"I have bought a sapphire," I said, without preamble. "I know it is real, but I do not know its exact value. Would you be so kind as to advise me?"

The great man was only too delighted. He examined the stone through a powerful magnifying glass, turned it in every direction, and ended by placing it on a balance that marked its weight to a milligram. His expression when he had finished was significant.

"You have a very old stone there," he said. "The cutting dates from several centuries ago, and was executed with primitive tools. I can offer you . . ."

I will not give the figure, but only say that its size made me blush. I declined his offer and left the shop. From there I went to a leather-worker and bought a morocco case with a secure fastening. I placed the sapphire in it, the case was hidden in a secret pocket in my waistcoat and never left my person.

Three weeks later I was back in India with its mountains. A thousand feet above the sea I had found a village, or rather an agglomeration of sordid bungalows. Among them were a few buildings constructed on the European plan, some wooden pavilions for tuberculous soldiers, and a little, fairly comfortable hotel, kept by a Swiss. I had difficulty in getting a room, for during the season a large number of tourists and pilgrims visit the place, which is celebrated for its temples. These are hewn out of the solid rock and are within easy reach of the mountains. They are accessible and visitors are well received. It was because of this, perhaps, that I felt impelled to visit another, a temple which is rarely seen. It also attracted me because it contained the most secret of the sanctuaries of the statue of Jaina, that gentle and ascetic Hindu who imposed on his disciples the respect for all life, human and animal.

I had already been warned that the temple was very difficult of access. To reach it one had to scramble up slopes of dry earth that crumbles like clinker under the hoofs of the mules. Moreover, a stranger would do better than to take the risk. Without being very precise the warnings

# ACCESSORY

of travelers, guides, and the European inhabitants of the country are distinctly discouraging.

My host, however, was more explicit.

"Do not go up there, sir," he said. "They tell of someone who went and never came back."

"That is apt to happen in the mountains," I retorted. "You, who are Swiss, ought to know that. But do not be afraid, I shall be prudent. Have a good, well-shod mule ready for me tomorrow morning at eight o'clock."

By eight next day I had passed through the village which was still sleeping behind its bamboo shutters. In front of me spread the country of the high plateaus, a sea of rough tilled earth, its fields burned by the sun and broken incessantly by the rusty domes of the hills. A road, like the dried-up bed of a river, passed between two rows of trees, the leaves of which were shriveled and dying, and on this expanse, which was the color of a dead leaf, a sky like unpolished glass threw an equal, continuous, and implacable heat. It resembled a late autumn undergoing all the extremes of summer. The road, which the mules covered slowly, approached the mountain by degrees and ended in a stony, circuitous path that climbed the flank of the hill. My mount attacked it resolutely. No doubt he knew the path. The ascent was lonely as well as arduous and I heaved a sigh of relief when the mule stopped suddenly at a plateau. It seemed as if he knew that this was the end of the journey. Had he carried the stranger who never came back? I did not linger on this thought, and there was enough that was strange before my eyes to distract me.

I had halted at the foot of a rocky barrier, pierced by an arch like the door of a Roman church. Through it one could see a dark, narrow passage. On each side, standing about a yard from the ground and touching the door, was a table of stone, and on each table sat six men dressed in peplums which had once been white but which were now a yellowish gray like the dust of the road. They were motionless, their arms and legs crossed, and their lowered eyes fixed on the ground. At my approach they did not move or raise their eyes. I might have been invisible.

I had dismounted and was standing hesitating when a monk, who had been hidden until now in the shadows of the passage, appeared suddenly and approached me. He was bearded and wore a turban. His features were fine and regular and his eyes sparkling.

"What do you want?" he asked in English, without returning my greeting.

"I should like to visit the temple and see the statue of Jaina," I answered.

He remained silent for a moment, examining me with such attention that one would have thought he was trying to fix my appearance in his memory. At last he made up his mind.

"Take off your shoes," he said briefly.

When I had done so the bonze led me into the passage, walking behind me on my heels. A little daylight filtered through the cracks in the rock, and at the end of the passage a confused light streamed through a second opening like the first. I drew back politely to give place to my guide.

"Go first," he ordered in a rough voice.

I obeyed.

I found myself in a vast, circular, windowless chamber; a diffused light came from an opal lamp hanging from the center of the arched roof. I could see the walls, on the stone of which swarmed a medley of animals, plants, and men, and the vaulted roof, covered with a network like the web of a gigantic and insane spider. At the end of the room was a niche and in it an alabaster statue, life-size, its legs crossed and hands clasped and its body constellated with jewels that glistened in the wavering light. At its feet were scattered faded flowers.

I was a couple of feet from the statue when I was suddenly seized by the elbows and dragged roughly back.

"Not so close," growled the bonze.

The light was better on the spot where he had placed me, and I could see a round face with the omniscient smile of Hindu divinities. In the right eye was a blue orbit consisting of a sapphire starred exactly like mine. The left orbit was empty.

"Your statue has only one eye," I said in surprise.

The answer fell heavily, word by word, in the silence.

"Two months ago someone came to the temple and stole the stone."

My hand went instinctively to my waistcoat. Something burned there

# ACCESSORY

against my chest. I had the sapphire that was stolen and I was about to give it back.

I have asked myself since what guardian angel prompted me to ask the question that saved two heads from a terrible vengeance.

"Do you know the thief?" I asked.

The priest of Jaina did not answer immediately. His body erect, his head lifted, and his eyes raised as though in prayer, he spoke in a loud voice, in a language I did not understand. Then, without looking at me, he translated, word for word, what he had been saying to the statue.

"One day Jaina will command the thief to return the stone. On that day the thief will return to the temple, and from that day onward he will never leave the temple again."

My hand that was not too steady came out of the pocket into which it had plunged. As it rose it came in contact with the still-fresh gardenia that I had placed in my buttonhole before I started on my journey. That flower I placed among the others at the feet of Jaina. This mute homage seemed to please the bonze. He smiled faintly.

That very night I left the mountain.

I did not give back the sapphire. I shall never return it. But if I am offered a fortune I shall never sell it.

# In the Cemetery at Scutari

*I* was on the point of leaving Istanbul, one of the loveliest places in the world, and I was glad to have had the opportunity of admiring its tarnished splendors before they vanished forever. On the day of my departure I felt a desire to see once more the cemetery at Scutari.

"Once more" is a figure of speech, seeing that I had never been there. But in the room in which I spent the first fifteen years of my life there was a picture by Emile David of the shores of an arm of the sea, intersected by the silhouettes of somber trees. White stones stood among these trees and the scene was a grim one. It was this that I wanted to see again.

Will anyone, I wonder, question my assertion that childish impressions have something of the permanence and grandeurs of eternal things? Or that the illusions of our very early days leave more profound traces than those born of the experiences of ten or fifteen years later? Every evening I entered that cypress wood. I walked there placidly and at length, and when I had reached its innermost recesses, I went to sleep there. In those days I believed that I knew every path and thicket. I imagined it as a silent and, above all, a deserted forest. An adventure was waiting for me there, however. One that I was not to comprehend until it was over.

Fifty years have passed since the days when Scutari knew my great-uncle and his paint brushes, and the town has spread itself. Today it penetrates into the interior of the cemetery, from which it used to be separated by cultivated fields and a tract of common land. In this intermediary zone wooden houses have been constructed for the officers of the garrison. Between these houses two or three cypresses act as enclosures. The houses spread out more and more, the trees increase in number, and at the end of a few minutes the pedestrian finds himself in the heart of the cemetery. The town of the living has merged insensibly into the town of the dead.

In what remains of this last a crowd circulates and its attitude astonishes those tourists who are ignorant of Eastern customs. For the Mussulman does not fear death and he likes the shade and coolness of the tombs. The Oriental has made that which in the West we call the House of Rest into a public garden where the people walk, eat, and chatter. Children play at hopscotch with little birdlike cries. Whole families have settled down there. They share slices of pink watermelon and *rissoles* wrapped in vine leaves and, seated on the rich grass of the tombs, their backs propped against the tombstones, they find that life is good.

Every now and then a woman passes. She is painted and she throws a sidelong glance at a solitary walker. They disappear together in the direction of a thicket that hides a dilapidated tomb. In the paradise promised to the sons of the Prophet death opens its arms to carnal love.

Farther on there is complete solitude, and it was here that I rediscovered the silent wood of my picture. But the trees had grown larger; their crowns met and were so closely interwoven as to exclude almost all daylight. Tombs were infrequent in this place, and it seemed almost as if, instead of planting trees beside the gravestones, solid blocks of marble, delicately carved with a turban in the case of a man, or with a bouquet of flowers in that of a woman, had been propped at random against the trunks of the cypress trees. These glistened in the glaucous shadow like lost flagstones seen under sea water.

A place forgotten. This part of the cemetery, older and more beautiful than the other, seems dedicated to abandonment and oblivion. Nobody troubles to clean the paths or keep them in decent condition, and I discovered with a shock that I was actually walking on the bones that lay across my path.

"Yet another tomb violated for the construction of their abominable barracks," I thought, with disgust.

But my ill-humor did not last long. I came out into a clearing where a thousand drunken nightingales were singing their loudest, and I stopped to hear them better and to admire the first star, shining in a patch of citron sky.

# IN THE CEMETERY AT SCUTARI

It was then that I discovered that I was not alone.

My companion was an animal, a dog. Its neck stretched out toward the human debris on the ground, it sniffed at the bones, then it approached me and stood motionless at my side.

I had time to examine, and even admire, it at my leisure. Standing fairly high on its legs, with gray-brown coat, its ears pointed and pricked and its slightly oblique eyes, it was an elegant beast. It gave me a curious feeling that I had seen it somewhere before. It was a mongrel, born of two breeds that I knew I should never succeed in tracing. Just one of those numerous curs that the inhabitants of Constantinople try in vain to get rid of.

I walked on. The dog followed me at a distance of five or six feet. I stopped, and the dog stopped too. I moved again, and once more it followed me. Once or twice it became bold enough to sniff at my clothes, then it kept its distance respectfully again.

Dogs like being spoken to, so I addressed my new companion. I asked him his name, where he came from, and whether he understood French, and told him not to scratch himself. He listened to my remarks, observing me the while, and continued to follow me.

Suddenly, around the corner of a path another dog appeared. It seemed almost as if it had been spying on me. Though larger and dirtier, it was exactly like the other, which he proceeded to join. Both began to trot discreetly at my heels.

I tried to make friends with the newcomer.

"You would be the better for a wash," I remarked. "And none the worse for a collar. Shall I buy you a green one with gold studs?"

The dog seemed to appreciate the suggestion of a collar. He leaned against me and sniffed with an audacity that seemed excessive. I gave him a fillip on the nose that drove him off, and he sprang back sharply, still keeping his eyes on me.

"No familiarities, please," I said. "If you want to make friends you can begin by taking a bath."

Intimidated either by the flip or my words, the dog drew back still farther and I walked on.

I heard a rustling in the bushes and two more dogs, like the first, appeared. Then another couple and, after them, still more. They emerged from the clumps of trees and the paths, came and sniffed me, and adopted me.

After a time I halted. There were eleven now, all alike, all miserable, dirty, and sad, and all strangely, obstinately faithful. They followed me with muted steps, steps so light that they stole like shadows, until the whole pack seemed but one dog.

From time to time I stopped to speak to them. They, too, stopped, in a body. Motionless, their eyes riveted on me, they listened. It was then that I observed a peculiarity that had hitherto escaped me. From the moment of our first encounter not one of them had wagged his tail. They were odd, these dogs of Constantinople.

I hurried on, for the dusk was falling, and my boat was due to leave that evening. From time to time I turned my head to throw a word to the eleven beasts that followed me so silently. Each time I did so I saw their eyes gleaming in the darkness of the shadows. As I looked back for the last time I stumbled over a root and nearly measured my length. I managed to grab a branch and, with an effort, haul myself upright. The whole thing lasted perhaps five seconds, but I had heard the sudden bound behind me, and when I swung around the whole pack, their fangs showing, were at my heels. They recoiled at once in one movement.

I addressed them in a speech worthy of one of the heroes of the classics.

"You are stout fellows! If I had fallen you would have come and licked my face and hands! You are good dogs and I should like to adopt the lot of you, but I cannot. I can take only one and I should like that one to be not too young, too old, too hairy, or too mangy. The fact is that you are all so ugly that it would be very difficult to choose between you!"

I had got to this point when a newcomer appeared at the end of the path. Though it was already dark I could distinguish the uniform and flat beret of a Turkish soldier. He was walking in my direction, and at the sight of me stopped as if petrified. Was it my flock that caused him such surprise?

I had no time to decide. The man plunged his hand into his belt, drew out an object I did not recognize, and leveled it at me. There was a shot, and a ball whistled past my ear. Two of the dogs lay dying at my feet. The others had fled. The soldier put up his revolver and ran toward me, apostrophizing me in a hoarse voice and gesticulating like a madman.

# IN THE CEMETERY AT SCUTARI

After a minute, realizing that I did not understand a word he was saying, he took me by the arm and dragged me in the direction of Scutari. As for the dogs that lay gasping and bloodstained on the grass, he took no notice of them.

We were soon back in the town, in the midst of belated walkers on their way home. The soldier relaxed his grip. He evidently meant me no harm. But I felt furious with him. He had just brutally killed two inoffensive animals that seemed to have taken a fancy to me, and had intervened, with the utmost savagery, in an affair that did not concern him at all. I told him all this in French. His French was as bad as my Turkish and he did not understand me, but he could see that I was angry, and showed a surprise that ended by bewildering me.

And this was not the last of my surprises. He kept on addressing the passers-by, evidently describing what had happened, and the effect of this recital exceeded anything I could have imagined. A Turkish crowd is not normally demonstrative, but it began to overwhelm us both, myself in particular, with expressions of sympathy. A stranger pressed my hand. He was followed by another. An old woman picked up the hem of my coat and kissed it, which embarrassed me profoundly. A young mother placed her baby in my arms, and, when I hastily returned it to her, thanked me, with looks and gestures, as if I had brought it back from the dead. And this crowd that pursued me, surrounded me, and touched my clothes, went on increasing. I became more and more the object of attention. Provoked and disconcerted, I hastened my steps, anxious to reach the jetty and the boat that would release me from this absurd position.

The soldier had dropped my arm, but he was still with me. He hurried up to the officer in charge of the gangway and spoke to him, pointing to me as he did so. The officer's jaw dropped and he stared at me. The soldier, having said his say, came back to me, and, bringing his hand first to his forehead then to his heart, departed at last, leaving me more puzzled than ever. Perhaps the gangway officer would be able to explain matters.

At least he spoke Italian and was able to translate the soldier's account. He spoke volubly, his eyes starting out of his head.

"This man was in the forest when he came suddenly on a stranger who was talking to a dozen wolves of whom he was not frightened. On this same road, a few days before and just a little farther on, these wolves had eaten a woman. The remains of her skeleton are still there. The soldier fired, killed two of the wolves, and put the others to flight. And at that the stranger became very angry."

I took in the words that followed, vaguely.

"A great saint . . . A Messenger from the Prophet . . . He has healed a little child . . . Wild beasts listen to him and do him no harm."

My memory had suddenly gone back fifteen years. My father had just returned from a journey in the French provinces and, at a hunting dinner, was repeating the words of an old *berrichon* postman.

"When I cross the forest with my letters, monsieur, I am always followed at a distance of ten feet by five or six wolves. They are waiting for me to fall. So long as I am on my feet they do not dare attack me, and, until now, I have never fallen. But I know that if ever I do fall it will be the end of me."

A few minutes later I was standing on deck under the lights of the boat. A steward was passing among the passengers, his slip of paper in his hand.

"Monsieur will take the dinner?" he asked.

"I shall not dine. Bring me a glass of rum."

# An Apparition

WHEN a writer wishes to plunge his readers, if he has any, into an atmosphere inducive of fear and charged with mystery, he takes care to place the characters of his story on a proper stage. He conjures up at will a lonely country house, or, what is even more nerve-racking and much more distinguished, an exaggeratedly medieval historical castle. Then, having thus provided for the first necessities, he unlooses the elements. His lightnings herald the crash of thunder, the rain beats against the windows, squalls of wind unexpectedly burst open the stoutest doors, and the sound of the sad sea waves, artfully compared to the cries of the wounded on the battlefield, complete the picture.

In view of this I am afraid that I shall have some difficulty in impressing on my readers one of the most profound and unique experiences of my life. For honesty compels me to conduct them to the heart of a large and very animated town, clangorous with the horns of the motors that pass, like a river in flood, down the wide streets; a town which even the night cannot make mysterious, for mystery flees before the blinding streamers of its electric signs and the perpetual glamour of its illuminated shop windows.

I am speaking of Zurich.

Not far from the Peterskirche there is a little restaurant well known to gourmets. For the benefit of those who may be attracted to it by greed or curiosity, I will say that the shutters are hatched with green and white, and that from its windows one can see not only the church of St. Peter, but also the charming house, now the parsonage, which once was the home of Lavater.

I have often mounted the oak staircase that leads to an ancient-looking room where one eats the wild duck that is worthy of its celebrity, a celebrity I have often deplored when I have found myself obliged to turn back, left in the lurch because I have omitted to order a table.

This staircase is separated from the exterior by a screen of frosted glass, decorated with bunches of grapes, in the center of which is a fairly good engraving representing Goethe at the age of fifty.

Some portrait of the poet is to be found almost everywhere in this house. A miniature has perpetuated the features of his youth, a sanguine chalk drawing the grave beauty of his riper days. Finally, a portrait of the school of Tischbein shows us an imposing old man, dressed in a greatcoat and wearing an immense hat, the brim of which does not completely hide his long "pepper-and-salt" hair. The master stands before a table, leaning upon it with his right hand, a long, delicate hand, bearing on the middle finger an enormous turquoise cut in a crescent, and that hand alone reveals the poet, aesthete, and writer.

This house remains faithful to the memory of Goethe. He often dined here. These stairs have creaked under his tread. At one of these tables he has sat, and here he has tasted in turn the wines of the Rhine and the Rhone. He has eaten the cream cheese of central Switzerland, and the apple fritters, the receipt for which has been so carefully preserved and which are still served with those fried cakes, covered with powdered sugar, that we call in French Switzerland "Merveilles," and which indeed sometimes merit the name. But I must apologize for this long digression and pass on to the incident that I am about to describe.

Only a few months ago I stopped for a night at Zurich.

Force of habit, joined to the more imperious urge of greed, led me to mount the staircase of polished wood once again.

As soon as I arrived I noticed that the illumination was bad. The electric bulbs burned like night lights. In that semi-obscurity the little room regained the rather severe aspect that it must have had a hundred years ago when it was lighted only by candles.

I remarked on it to the maid.

"It is the first time it has happened," she said. "And it has come at a good time, seeing that there is no one here."

"What, no one?"

"No one," she declared again. "And it is very extraordinary. It is the first time such a thing has happened in the fifteen years I have been here."

# AN APPARITION

In truth, though the tables were laid and a few chairs fallaciously turned up gave an illusion of business, I was, in fact, the only guest of the house and I remained so, or very nearly.

While I struggled inelegantly, but victoriously, with my frogs' legs, I noticed that little by little the street noises were becoming deadened.

There were no more motor horns, no roaring of engines, not even the sound of footsteps. Gradually silence invaded the room, and its progression was so regular that I began to wonder, not without apprehension, whether it was not a subjective phenomenon, due to deafness on my part.

The noisy arrival of the maid with the stuffed mushrooms I had ordered reassured me.

"It is snowing hard," she said. "The flakes are so thick that you cannot see a yard ahead. That is why the light is so bad. They say that the cables break when they have to support a heavy load of fresh snow."

I got up, went to the window, drew aside the curtains, and looked out. The snow was falling in thick flakes.

Their silent avalanche muffled little by little all the noises of the town.

From the Peterskirche the cracked bell of the clock tolled ten strokes in the silence, and suddenly, in that badly lighted room, with sounds from the streets silenced, I imagined myself transported back a hundred and fifty years. The very voice of the antique clock seemed like a sigh of resigned old age.

All at once I heard a sound which I did not expect, an anachronism which fitted in well with my reverie. It was the tinkling of bells, accompanied by the muffled rhythm of a carriage and pair. I listened, but I was not mistaken.

The noise approached, becoming more and more distinct. I could even have sworn that the invisible equipage (I had looked out of the window in the hope of seeing it) had stopped at the door of the inn.

It is, I reflected, the mail of the old days. It used to stop here to change horses. Unless it is a phantom coach.

The stairs creaked under the weight of a firm and measured tread. Then the footsteps grew near and the door opened.

A tall man entered the room. He was wearing a greatcoat that resembled a "houppelande," and his head was crowned by a wide-brimmed hat caked with snow.

He took off his coat and hat, threw a rapid glance at the portrait by Tischbein, and seated himself. I remained stupefied.

I saw before me, under the portrait, its exact but living replica. The same aquiline nose, the same long pepper-and-salt hair, the same haughty carriage of the thrown-back head, and a detail that seemed incredible, the same starched cravat, of a style that has now vanished, supporting the chin and overlapping it with the two points.

The maid had fetched the menu and placed it in front of him. Then, at last, he took off his gloves.

I saw a long, nervous hand, with sensitive fingers. The middle one bore an enormous turquoise cut in a crescent.

For a moment I wondered if I was dreaming. A sudden improvement in the light convinced me that I was wide awake. The individual really was there. Installed in his corner, he was peacefully pursuing his meal. And all the time he was eating I never ceased to look at him.

At first he did not seem to notice this, then his eyes, in a moment of absence, caught mine, and I thought I surprised a slightly mocking smile on his lips. Then, without taking any further notice of me, he finished his dinner. When he had done he put on his greatcoat, hat, and gloves, asked for the bill, bestowed on the maid a smile that deserved a curtsey, and departed, very quickly, without a word, as though he were afraid of being interrupted. I heard his rapid descent of the stairs. The entrance door opened, shut again, and the noise of the bells sounded outside.

I hastily paid for what I had eaten and rushed into the kitchen.

"Who was the gentleman who just went out?" I demanded of the proprietor, who was busy with his saucepans.

My voice must have sounded strange, for he hesitated for an instant before answering.

"He is a gentleman from Weimar," he said at last. "He came back tonight to assist at the opening of an exhibition that is being held in honor of his great-grandfather, Wolfgang Goethe."

Shortly afterward I left and was lucky enough to find a sledge, the snow having made the roads impossible for motors. And, enveloped in the goatskin that served as a rug, my eyes closed, I listened with pleasure to the silver laughter of the sleigh bells.

They seemed as though they were mocking at our civilization.

# The Visitation

MY FRIEND Gabrielle is an angel. But let me make this quite clear. She is a modern angel, even a worldly one.

She wears hats signed by Rose-Valois and Marie-Alphonsine, and her white hair is tinted a shade of pale heliotrope. It is cut short and worn so as to reveal an ear ornamented with a great black pearl.

Gabrielle reads all the latest novels, and more than once well-known authors who appreciated her judgment and delicacy of taste have sent her the manuscripts of their unpublished works.

She often plays bridge and more often poker. If San Remo were not so far from Rome she would play, even more often, roulette. And if I add that Gabrielle is now close on seventy you will agree that she deserves to be called both modern and worldly.

Just so, you will answer, but how does this make an angel of her? Roulette, not to mention fashionable hats and black pearls, do not justify the qualification.

But wait a minute. These things that I have told you are the venial sins of Gabrielle, and many of the people who think they know her, know only of these. If you asked them how she spent her mornings they would open their eyes and answer in astonishment: "How? In the same way as all other elegant women. Her bath, the masseuse, the hairdresser, beauty culture, correspondence, and the perusal of *Vogue* occupy the time for her, as for all the others between ten o'clock in the morning, when she opens her eyes, till one when she lunches."

But they would be wrong. This is how Gabrielle passes her mornings:

At seven o'clock, in winter as well as in summer, she takes a cold shower, brushes her hair vigorously, puts on an old coat and skirt of

Scotch tweed, and tops it with a head-covering that no longer has a right to any precise denomination. She then arms herself with a carpetbag that resembles those of her grandparents. Thus equipped she walks with her characteristically short, rapid steps in the direction of the poorest quarters in Rome.

The contents of that carpetbag are amazing. Sulphate of quinine for Sor Antonio, an ex-toll collector, who suffers from malaria; aspirin tablets for old Mancini, who is guardian of the Cemetery of San Lorenzo, and who complains that the dead pass on their rheumatism to him; bandages of sterilized lint to renew the dressings of Zia Elvira, who has burned her left foot by upsetting on it, by mistake, a cup of boiling oil with which she was trying to destroy bugs. Gabrielle herself removes the purulent compress and replaces it with a new dressing.

In this bag are also cotton handkerchiefs. She distributes these to afflicted mothers (in Italy they would call them blessed) of brats that are too numerous to get their noses blown. There are also tins of cocoa for the nourishment of underfed children, and bags of tapioca for invalids. Often when there is no stove, Gabrielle herself teaches her protégées how to prepare their soup on an oil lamp. From this bag she produces bottles of malt which she reserves for nursing mothers, licorice for coughing children (and there is a chorus of coughing as soon as she appears), and, last of all, holy images.

These go to the despairing, those who have nothing more to hope from medicine or the doctor. In those cases in which man can only complain or hold his tongue, the angels intercede for him.

The images that Gabrielle carries always represent Saint Theresa of Lisieux. You may think that, as a Huguenot, I might take exception to what the skeptics sometimes scornfully designate as "bondieuseries." You are mistaken; I believe that they help people, and this is why.

In my room, facing my bed, is a landscape. When I am ill I look at it. My imagination roams in the woods or along the river and I suffer less. And if the sight of a landscape has the power to assuage one's pains and ease one's sorrows, why deny this power to the mild face of a saint or perhaps, who knows, to an invisible presence?

It has often been my lot to surprise Gabrielle entering some sordid house, the almost bursting carpetbag on her arm. When she emerged

# THE VISITATION

later she would roll it on itself and carry it like a field marshal's baton. If, by chance, it was not empty I would see her make her way to another dwelling and attack another rickety stair. And she would continue thus, performing her angelic task, until she had nothing more to give.

One day I confessed to her that I had been the involuntary witness of her charities. I expressed my admiration of this untiring and secret pilgrimage. And I added, very tactlessly, I admit, that she would be rewarded either in this world or the next.

"I have already had my reward," she answered. "And it was all the more beautiful because it came at a moment when I did not in the least deserve it."

I was about to protest, but she forestalled me.

"No, it is not what you think. But since you have touched on a subject that I have so much at heart, I will tell you a true story. Would it bore you too much to hear it at my house?"

I relieved my old friend of her carpetbag, and accompanied her to her home at the top of the Janiculum. As she is as hospitable as she is charitable, she ordered for me a liqueur of which I have forgotten the name. I only know that it is prepared according to a recipe that is very old and almost unknown, and that the Medicis tasted its flavor of incense and muscatel. My hostess took just enough to keep me company. When her glass was empty she rose, found a key which seemed to be cunningly hidden in a drawer, opened a secretaire, and drew out a box. With another key, as carefully concealed as the first, she opened the box. What treasure, what relic could be hidden in it?

Gabrielle had reseated herself. She sat for a moment in silence, looking at a stout envelope of white linen which she held in both hands. At last, with infinite precaution, as though she were afraid of breaking it, she placed it on the table.

"You think, perhaps, that I am rewarded by the gratitude of all these poor people," she said. "Indeed, that would be enough to make me happy. But it is rarely that they receive me with anything but complaints and recriminations. Things are always getting worse with them, and when they are going better they find my visits intrusive. Then they receive me coldly. At a pinch they will even make me feel that I am being indiscreet. I ought not to let this bother me. In reality that frame of mind is so excusable. These poor people have the mentality of children. It hurts them to expose their sufferings to the eyes of the rich, yet, on the other hand, they feel that the rich hardly do even their duty in giving them crumbs that fall from their table, and, after all, is not that true? But the heart has its weaknesses. One day when the sirocco was blowing, I had almost broken my back climbing broken stairs and visiting sordid hovels. I had been badly received and, I think, even exploited without scruple. When people are miserable the temptation is so strong! When at last I arrived home I fell into a chair exclaiming:

" 'Oh, most gracious Father! Never an affectionate word, never a smile of recognition, or a sign of gratitude! And yet, how that would help me in my daily task!'

"I was still speaking when I heard the sound of the doorbell. The maid answered it, and announced that a nun was asking to see me. Today I tremble to think that in that moment of despair I was on the point of saying that I was at home to no one. That formula that one would do well to dispense with.

" 'Ask her in,' I said, with an impatient sigh. 'Show her into the drawing room and ask her name.'

"A moment later the maid returned.

" 'The sister is in the drawing room. She says that Madame knows her well. She is called Sister Theresa.'

" 'Sister Theresa!' I exclaimed in astonishment. 'You must be mistaken, or else you did not hear her properly. I know several nuns, but none of them bear the name of Theresa.'

" 'Madame, I am certain that that was the name. But Madame can see for herself.'

"I went downstairs to the drawing room. It was empty.

"Very much surprised, I searched the adjoining rooms. They, too, were empty. I rang for the maid.

" 'Rosine, where is the nun?'

"Rosine looked round her.

" 'I will look next door,' she said at last.

" 'I have already done so, but you can try.'

"Rosine repeated my investigations, without success, and came back.

" 'Madame,' she declared, 'I left the sister sitting on this sofa.'

"In effect a crushed cushion was witness to the fact that someone had recently leaned against it. Rosine was lost in thought. All at once she left the room, leaving the door open, and went straight to the front door. I followed her.

" 'Madame can see? The door is locked on the inside.'

" 'Are you quite sure there is no one in the apartment?'

" 'No one, madame, I have been everywhere.'

"I went back to the drawing room feeling perplexed and, I admit, a little anxious. Involuntarily I looked at the sofa. On a table close to it there was a small white rose.

"I remembered then the words of Saint Theresa on her deathbed: 'After my death I will cause a rain of roses to fall upon the earth.' "

Gabrielle opened the envelope and took out what had once been a rose, now a bunch of faded and yellowed petals.

"Here is the rose of Saint Theresa. It has kept its scent. Every time I smell it I think of how little good I have done and of all I can still do. And I tell myself that I have been marvelously rewarded."

A faint perfume still floated round the envelope from the faded flower. Shortly afterward I took my leave.

Am I wrong in saying that Gabrielle is an angel?

# The Leaning Rock

Set up at the junction of two roads, one of which runs from Davos Dorf, the other from Davos Platz, it overhangs the Schatzalp. Were its base not solidly embedded, this block, leaning like the Tower of Pisa, could easily, on a windy day, reach Davos in a few strides, crushing on its route the gold cock shining from the steeple of the parish church.

I have looked often and long at this strange stone standing in the center of a majestic alpine landscape.

Seen from a distance it dominates the deep furrows of valleys, the sloping pastures, the waves of granite breaking against the horizon. As you approach the rock you will observe at its base a kind of shelter, and if you enter this vault you will discover a cavity in the wall, easily big enough to admit a human body.

At the beginning of my stay at Davos this shelter did not treat me kindly. Twice I climbed the Schatzalp. Surprised by rain, I sought refuge under the rock. The cavity in which I hoped to take refuge was occupied on both occasions. Twice in a single week I found the same person crouching in the retreat, and, to all appearances, in no way disposed to share it.

The stranger was youthful in appearance. At first sight his harsh and tightened face displeased me. I noted the too symmetrical profile and the man's air of belonging to a dying race. At the second meeting I became aware that the stranger was an invalid. Sickness seemed to have dissolved all the flesh of that incorporeal face in which only the transparent complexion and the wonderful eyes survived. This was not the end of a race but the end of a life.

Two summers passed. I had completely forgotten the stranger of the Schatzalp, when one day a sudden association of images reminded me of him.

It happened that I was crossing the Strela Pass which separates Davos from Arosa. Already I could see the lake of Davos set in the landscape like a blue butterfly in a field. A sharp turn of the road and the silhouette of the rock rose before me, and with it the image of the stranger whom I had twice found crouched in the stone vault. Was he still alive? Would I ever see him again?

Hardly had I posed this question when I saw him. Disregarding the main road and following a footpath across the fields, he was going, it seemed to me, toward the rock. I had not expected so prompt a reply and I was suddenly aware that I was on the point of uncovering a secret guarded by the rock.

I have never been able to resist the temptation to solve a mystery. Ten feet away there was copse; I hid there. I wanted to see without being seen.

Clearly the stranger's sickness had progressed. He walked slowly, and with great effort. When he reached the rock he stopped, stared at it fixedly, and stood motionless. A minute of this, and I began to wonder whether I might not be in the presence of a madman.

The man was talking to the stone. Not only did he speak to it, but he went up to it and began to stroke it tenderly, as one caresses a child or an invalid. At last he rested his head against it, murmuring words the sense of which I could not catch. It was as though he were whispering in the ear of some invisible being.

I slipped away without his seeing me. I was amazed, of course, but less curious than troubled. Doubtless I had surprised some tender secret by my trick. This stone, so dear to a sufferer close to death, must be the altar to some memory.

Some days afterward I received a letter with a German postmark. A young woman, with whom I had become acquainted when I stayed in that country, had learned that I was at Davos, and had written to ask me to visit a sick Austrian friend at the sanatorium, who had not replied to her last letters.

Was he still at the sanatorium? Was he suffering too severely for him to write? Perhaps he was dead?

My correspondent sent me what information she had, her friend's room number and the name of his physician.

The sanatorium occupied the highest point of the valley. Surrounded by silence, protected by parks at each turn of the road and at each forest outlet, the enormous structure dominated the view with its long white mass, shaped like a horseshoe. It raised heavenward its four identical balconies, striped with regularly spaced supporting columns, which, seen from a distance, seemed to transform the balconies into cells. One might have conceived the edifice a prison built by a philanthropist. There was only one place in the whole valley where the lay of the land and the entanglement of trees hid the sanatorium from view.

I had no desire to enter it. The call I was asked to pay had no temptations for me.

But how was I to refuse such a request? That afternoon I walked leisurely to the sanatorium. I knew that I could not just knock at the door and be admitted. As it turned out, in order to visit a patient one had to conform to specific rules of protocol, rules even more elaborate than I had imagined.

To the right, on entering, were the quarters of the concierge, separated from the vestibule by a balustrade.

The occupant, a man about forty years old, had the breadth of shoulder, the close-cropped head, the definite speech and bearing of a ship's officer. And he wore a dark blue uniform. However, the symbol embroidered with gold thread above the lapel of his round jacket was not a ship's anchor, but a jailer's key. The wall behind him was checkered with cubbyholes. In these tiny compartments, each of which had a given number, various letters, messages of love, pity, anguish, and hope, waited to be distributed.

The concierge consulted a list posted on the wall, then he took me into their lobby and told me to wait.

There was a strangling odor of creosote. Very faint in the vestibule and in the office of the concierge, which were constantly aired by the comings and goings of visitors and guards, the smell filled the corridor and seeped into the lobby. Now, even when it does not remind you of death and disease, the smell of creosote is unpleasant.

Brown and yellow dominated the color scheme of the lobby. There were tobacco-colored leather chairs and dark mahogany tables supported by legs of washable and aseptic ebonite.

On the floor there were slabs of yellow marble. The stucco columns, whose reason for being there I could not imagine, were a poor imitation of the *giallo antico*. But there was one gay note in the otherwise total severity. A wreath of flowers and leaves hung from the shelf over the hearth. Personally, I would have preferred the coziness of a fire. But open fires are forbidden in sanatoriums; the patients might become too sensitive to cold if they became accustomed to warming themselves at a hearth. No rugs. Rugs accumulate germs.

There was nothing more to observe. What could I do to fill time?

Sky-blue circulars sprawled over one of the tables. Prospective inmates and their dear ones could find in these circulars all the information they desired. I leafed through one of these, idly.

Price of board . . . extras . . . additional fees. . . . Wonderful view of the valley, an inexhaustible source of pleasure. . . . During the winter, those inmates who are too weak to leave their beds can watch the skaters from the balcony. . . . The operating room is provided with the most modern installations. (Artificial pneumothorax. . . . Severing of interpulmonary adhesions. . . . Plates and covers disinfected, after using, by vapors and by thorough soaping. . . .) The family of the patient is regularly informed about his condition. . . . "Why do not they devote a paragraph to their superior burials?" I wondered.

Decidedly, philanthropy takes strange forms when based on science. I dropped the brochure back on the table as the concierge entered and offered to guide me to the lift.

I was led down two bright corridors with two high ceilings. Between walls rinsed with reseda, whose neutral shade leaves no stains, nurses and attendants all in white went back and forth, their footsteps evoking unexpected cadences in the empty spaces. I was reminded of a cathedral. One door after another, all closed, over each of them a number. What desire for violent life, how fierce a lust for freedom, must sometimes break loose among these men and women caught in the gears of this formidable machine!

We arrived at the third floor. The attendant in charge brought me to a room which led to a balcony. There, in the open, lying in a wheel bed, shaded by a rice-paper parasol whose brilliant gold lent him color, I beheld my mysterious visitor of the rock. His smile was cheery as he bade me sit. But when he had learned the reason for my visit he burst out, half-wearied, half-impatient:

"Yes, that is just like her! I received her last letter eight days ago and she demands a reply!"

"May I inform her that I have seen you, and that you appear to be in very good hands? May I assure her that you are going to write to her soon?"

"I would be in your debt if you informed her that you had seen me, and told her, too, that I have not forgotten her. But I cannot promise to write. It is better for me, considering what I have become, to break all the bonds that tie me to the world. I shall long for it less."

With all sincerity I made the conventional, the banal reply:

"But are you not exaggerating the seriousness of your condition? Only ten days ago I saw you in the Schatzalp. You must have walked a distance most people would consider extremely lengthy."

He raised his eyebrows.

"Yes . . . my excursion. But on that day I was there perhaps never to return."

I decided to be frank. I said:

"I do not wish to pry into your affairs. But I have several times seen you close by the rock. And I cannot but wonder why you have chosen this particular spot as the goal of your walks in the valley."

The sick man closed his eyes. It seemed to me that his pale cheeks became a faint pink. "Perhaps I shall tell you someday . . . not now." There was a moment of silence, then he resumed:

"It is frightening," he murmured, "that those of our acts which we believe to be most secret are known by someone whom we do not know."

He spoke without bitterness, he had not reproached me, but I felt the depth of his emotion. I quickly took my leave, not very proud of myself, but more than ever intrigued.

Several visits followed the one I have described. During our next conversation he told me his name and nationality. He was Karl Hellmuth, an Austrian.

A month passed. The time for me to leave the valley had arrived.

During my visits to the sanatorium neither Hellmuth nor I had once alluded to the secret of the rock, which I now regarded as a subject forbidden. I was resigned to carry in my memory a mystery, which, of all those mysteries which life had set for me would, perhaps, be the only one to remain unsolved.

What I had not counted on was the curious psychology of invalids. Sick men, who know their death is near, are, like travelers, subject to sudden bursts of confidence. They are ready to reveal their secrets to strangers, because they are certain they will never see them again.

On the eve of my departure I went to bid Hellmuth good-by.

I found him reclining, feverish, his eyes brilliant, his cheeks flushed. On the table beside his bed was a bouquet of cyclamen in a water glass, and this was surprising, for he had told me that he disliked flowers; their perfume disturbed him. He did not, as usual, greet me with a smile, but indicated with a movement of his hand that I should sit beside him.

"You are returning to Arosa? You are going through the Strela Pass? In that case . . ."

He hesitated a moment, and his flush became more marked.

"You could do me a great service. I am thinking of entrusting you with a mission."

"But I am ready to do anything you propose," I replied, moved by this request, and prompted, too, by what I sensed would be a decisive confidence.

"Would you take these flowers with you when you go? And"—he hesitated—"would you place them at the foot of the rock where we first met?"

The request baffled me, and I gave an involuntary start which he misinterpreted.

"Yes, I know it sounds nonsensical. But we Austrians are sentimental. People of other countries can never understand our cult of that humble flower, the 'forget-me-not.' You will say that flowers should be placed on graves. . . . Yes. . . . But it's just that. The rock is a grave."

He continued, his voice even and monotonous, without emphasis or resonance:

"When one feels the imminence of death—no, don't try to reassure me—when, I was saying, one feels the end is near, one is seized by a last desire. In spite of everything, a man would like to leave behind something dear to him in this world of the living. Something—oh, so little a thing—the memory of the one moment which was worth experiencing."

The moment of the first and ultimate confidence had come. In this room whose bare walls already presaged the strict emptiness of the grave, he recited, speaking in fits and starts, stopping only to get his breath, the following story:

"I came here four years ago. My illness was then in its first stages. But my chances looked good. I was assured that two years of careful treatment and I would be well again. I could return to my normal life in the city.

"After a few months I began to feel the benefits of a monkish life. They are right to impose that kind of regime on us. We accept it obediently, for we cannot but acknowledge that boredom and chastity are the two best physicians. And today I would be healthy and fit again if . . ."

He paused for a moment and turned his head away from me. He did not face me when he took up his story, and he spoke in a louder tone, as if he felt that he was defying his own sense of delicacy in not remaining silent.

"One evening a young woman checked in, a foreigner. What I mean to say is that she was not Austrian. I shall tell you her first name. It was Claire. How well she deserved that name! You should have seen her! I will not say that she was blonde. The word is too common. I know only one way to describe the nuance of her hair; it was like wintry gold. And in spite of the sickness that consumed her she was so gay, so merry! She brought joy to everyone near her. She came with her husband. What was he like? Devoted to her, there was no question about that, he was always with her, but his vulgarity made me shudder. No, I cannot accuse him of brutality, but the sheer grossness he betrayed when he spoke disgusted everybody. I met the new couple the evening they arrived. The husband then and there declared that he hated the mountains, adding:

" 'Still, I wouldn't care about making the sacrifice if I were certain that my wife would be saved.' And on another occasion he said in my presence to several of the inmates:

" 'I have become accustomed to acting only in terms of my wife's needs. I often wonder how I shall occupy myself when she is gone.' And the boor spoke in so loud a tone that not a word escaped his wife. She did not say anything, but her lips tightened.

"From the very beginning I pitied her. And what I want you to understand is that among people of sentiment there is hardly any distinction between pity and love. For one evening, with all my soul I bewailed an unfortunate. And then I knew that my heart no longer belonged to me.

"People speak of 'twin souls.' But this is a false and empty conception unless it applies to lovers. I see nothing in the fraternal relations of men which justifies such an idea. No . . . but for lovers it is valid. Before actually encountering the other, each has sought for and recognized the other. The same landscapes stir them. They respond to the same works of art. They vibrate to the sounds of the same musical theme, to the verses of the same poet. They enter into one another so completely that only death can pluck them apart. Before a month had passed, the two of us had reached this unity of sentiment. Even our silences spoke. And when her husband let slip some gross remark we turned away from each other, each trying to hide a blush of rage or shame.

"But in spite of everything I owe that man something. It was one of his hateful remarks that led to the climax. He was talking to one of the doctors, and, as usual, spoke at the top of his voice. Here is what he said:

" 'From now on I shall be rid of an illness from which I suffered much when I married: jealousy. Now the Koch bacillus stands like the sword of Siegfried between the lips of my wife and those of other men.'

"That very evening I kissed those ardent lips which now belonged only to me.

"I don't know how it was that we were able to meet and be alone with each other in the sanatorium. But it was not there that . . ."

He was quiet for a while and his cheeks were on fire. Reticence and respect for the absent loved one gave him pause. I understood his feeling.

He continued with a rush of words:

"We went out at the same time, late in the afternoon. The doctors were somewhat lax. For an hour or two we were free. To prevent suspicion we took different paths. And we met at a place which you know."

He became more and more excited.

"Free! We were free! We escaped this prison life! We outwitted the attendants and stole to our meetings! Up there in the rocky crypt we lived!"

There followed a pause which I was disinclined to break. Hellmuth, now somewhat calmer, went on:

"We returned to the sanatorium by different paths. And no one suspected. . . ."

Again a moment of silence. Hellmuth said:

"This went on for about two months. Then for a week I did not see her and I surmised that her illness had taken a turn for the worse. But I did not dare to ask after her. Someone remarked in passing that she had left the sanatorium. A few hours later I learned that she had died the previous night. At Davos death is never announced. To die is to disappear. She was gone without being able to leave me a single token of our intimacy. Nothing, you understand. Nothing to symbolize what is the only true sentiment of my life. Nothing, not a line of her writing, not a snapshot taken on the road by some itinerant photographer, not a lock of her hair, not a withered flower. And for this we alone were to blame. We refused to believe that we were going to die. We wished to do nothing that suggested coming grief. Alas, nothing remains of my vanished happiness. I could not even speak of her to anyone. Can one betray the secret of one who is dead? I was in an empty room in which I could find no trace of the perfume she shed.

"Nevertheless, something of her endures."

For the first time since he had begun his recital, Hellmuth looked me full in the face.

"You never entered the opening in the rock?"

I indicated that I had not. He said in low tones:

"If you enter it you will see on the left wall the imprint of her lips."

I thought he was delirious. He sensed as much, and without permitting me to interrupt him, recited the final episode of his love story.

One day a violent storm broke out and wind-lashed pellets of rain beat against the walls of the crypt. The spurts of water made dark stains on the slate-colored walls, and Hellmuth called this to the attention of his companion. She, laughing, pressed her lips against the stone. But the faint imprint was quickly effaced, and Hellmuth gave an exclamation of regret. Claire again kissed the cold stone wall, and, before the second imprint was blotted out, carefully underlined with the indelible lipstick women always carry with them the contours of her lips.

The sad recital was completed. Hellmuth closed his eyes. After a while he reopened them and looked at me.

"She was condemned," he said, "but I, I was reprieved. And now . . ."

A moment later I bade him good-by.

That very evening I placed the little bouquet at the foot of the rock and entered the crypt. It was quite dark, but after a while I was able to see.

Gradually, at the base of the rock, the outlines of a grave emerged from the obscurity.

But on the wall was the imprint of a little mouth, a mouth still smiling, a mouth with poisoned lips. . . .

Karl Hellmuth died six weeks after my departure.

/The Love-Letter

MY GUEST, a famous dancer, refused a tenth cigarette but took another cup of tea. Following the custom of his native Ruthenia, he put the lump of sugar I gave him under his tongue and sipped the bitter, amber fluid through it. Then he said:

"You have been present at what you are pleased to call my 'triumphs,' which you will allow me to rename 'successes.' My modesty, believe me, is genuine, and I am going to tell you the reason, a secret I have so far confided to no one. My chequered existence is not, I think, far from its end [politely I made a gesture of contradiction which he pretended not to see] and, in any case, the time has come to bring my career to a close. If what I am about to say were known, it could do me no harm from now on.

"Well... the real truth is this, that never... you understand, NEVER, during the forty years that I have been appearing on the stage the world over, have I had one single love-letter."

"That's easy to explain," I intervened. "Your admirers were persuaded in advance that you received so many, they were discouraged from trying their luck!"

But my friend shook his head. "No, no," he said, "your reasoning is wrong because for my partner things have been very different. She asked me, rather spitefully, to open the innumerable letters spread out in her dressing-room (especially when the writing on the envelope was unfamiliar to her). These letters, I must say, were all more or less alike: 'You do not know me and yet every day I am one of your audience, for since the time when I first saw you dance, I have had only one thought...'"

I tried again to reassure him. "If you have never had a letter like that," I argued, only half convinced, "it is just because women are more reserved than men. They are less expansive. Besides, seeing you always with the same partner, they have probably concluded that you are an indissoluble couple!"

"Perhaps," muttered the dancer, deep in thought. "This time I think I can follow your argument better. But," he began again after a minute or two, talking rather loud, as Russians do when they want to persuade you, "there ought to have been at least ONE exception . . . the exception with a capital E. There ought to have been ONE person who would have scorned the rules of decorum, one woman who would have written to me . . . as a last resource!"

I should have liked to console my dancer with his greying hair by saying that his own case was far from unique and that my career as an author had never brought me, either, a single love-letter. But such a confession would have been the less sincere in that every first of the month since the beginning of the year I had received a little mauve envelope (which I learned to recognise at a distance) containing a card, mauve also, inscribed with a brief message, always the same, and made up of three words: "I love you." No signature, no date, and of course no address . . . The stamp alone gave a vague clue; it was always postmarked at the Central Post-Office of Neuchâtel. But Neuchâtel has more than fifty thousand inhabitants; so the puzzle remained unsolved. I refrained from telling my friend about this "success" and he went away with his head down, rather depressed, I thought.

A little while after this conversation I happened to have a visit from a relation who often came to stay a day or two in my house. My cousin was a graphologist . . . quite a celebrated graphologist. So I took it into my head to show her one of the famous anonymous declarations. To my surprise, after glancing for a moment at the three words, so clearly written, she began to look embarrassed and, it seemed to me, a little suspicious. Obviously she was in no hurry to commit herself. In the end she made excuses. "It will only be tomorrow," she said, as if trying to gain time, "that I can give you my considered opinion." And she went off to her room, taking with her the short message which seemed so much to have displeased her.

# THE LOVE-LETTER

The next morning at breakfast it was she who began again about the notes, for I must confess that this small problem had escaped my mind, a further proof that I gave it little importance. With all the energy of shy people she burst out: "Here's a pretty kettle of fish! The message is written by a man!" And she handed me back the mauve card in an off-hand manner that seemed to me put on.

"By a MAN!" I exclaimed, or rather repeated.

"By a man; that is absolutely certain," went on my cousin, who appeared relieved of a great weight. "All the graphologists in the world would agree with me. But if it's any consolation to you," she continued almost at once, "I can tell you immediately that the author of this note is no . . ." She hesitated, looking for her words, ". . . is no whipper-snapper . . . no, this is the writing of a man of mature years, of an aristocrat with much experience of life, as you can see from the elegance of the script and a slight trembling which shows a tendency to Parkinson's disease or . . . a tremendous passion for yourself."

"I prefer the latter hypothesis," I answered, laughing. "It is more flattering. But you see I'm quite surprised to learn that at an age of increasing baldness I can inspire a tremendous passion (to use your own words) in some one of my own sex and mature years. It really is bewildering and makes me doubtful about the value of graphology. . . ."

"Of mature years is right," agreed my cousin without taking up my point about her art. "The letters he makes are those given as models to schoolboys at a time when the writing-master still trimmed goose quills for his pupils and taught them to make the flourishes that today are quite forgotten. As for the 'distinction' which I attribute to the author of these lines, or, more exactly, this line, I find it in the firmness of the writing, in the perfect formation of the *f* and the *s*, at one time so alike, as you might have noticed in examining original letters of Jean Jacques Rousseau. Indeed, this script reminds me a little of his."

"Well, well," I said to myself, "I had forgotten that she was a spiritualist. Perhaps she is going to attribute the origin of these messages to phenomena from the spirit world."

"Look, my dear," I went on after a moment, "supposing we admit that you have guessed the sex of my correspondent, could you not say more about his character, profession and personality?"

No doubt my cousin had spent a sleepless night making a thorough study of the writing in the mysterious message, for she knew her verdict by heart and recited it like a well-learnt lesson:

"An elderly person, fond of solitude, of the male sex, elegant, distinguished, but lacking in imagination. An egoist . . . so terrifically egoistic that I am even surprised to find him expressing feelings of . . . tenderness! As a matter of fact, everything goes to prove that this individual is in love only with himself . . . a perfect case of the narcissus complex. I will add that your correspondent is extraordinarily meticulous. Look at the dot on the *i*, absolutely round and placed exactly above the letter!"

"Oh, well," I said, laughing. "If I should inherit a fortune from my unknown . . . admirer, I won't fail to let you know, and there will even be something for you!"

My cousin seemed delighted that I had not taken her remarks too seriously. And no doubt the enquiry into the origin of the mauve cards would have remained where it was had it not been for the curiosity of a girl who came from time to time to see me, hoping for little presents to keep our friendship going . . . as her interest in me was not entirely disinterested. Unfortunately she fell on my collection of love-letters, and she was not going to pass over in silence a discovery which, she maintained, proved the existence of a rival on whom I doubtless showered most handsome gifts. The rival was trying to supplant her in my affections and she must put an end to this "odious" correspondence.

Luckily for her, and unluckily for me, she was very friendly with a professional detective. At first the expert was inclined to show her the door and return the two cards which she had produced as "tangible proof" of my "infidelity." Then, all at once, he thought better of it; the detective in him came to the surface.

"Unknowingly you have set before me a most disconcerting problem. These two cards have not been written on the same day nor with the same ink. Yet I could swear that they are exact reproductions of a third document which resembles them in every detail. Look how the words on both cards are alike! They could be laid exactly on top of one another like negative and positive films. Yet there is no question here of photographic material or even of sensitive paper."

# THE LOVE-LETTER

Then the detective scratched his chin with a puzzled air...

"In any case, this mauve paper seems to me uncommon enough and perhaps might furnish a clue to identify the sender. Would you trust me with one of the cards?"

"Gladly," answered the girl, whose curiosity was thoroughly aroused, and who would not have hesitated to lend the policeman the Eiffel Tower if she could be sure that this weighty document would have helped him to discover her rival, whose eyes she swore to tear out. "My friend will never notice that the card is gone. There is an incalcuable number of messages."

She exaggerated, since there were only four or five, but actually she was right because I did not notice the disappearance of the mauve card, taken from a drawer that I had not locked, having nothing, in fact, on my conscience.

A month went by without the detective, who had much else to think about, giving any sign of life. Then one day he telephoned Claudine (where women were concerned, he was too clever ever to write) to tell her that he had without the slightest difficulty found the shop which sold these elegant, old-fashioned cards. Only one customer came from time to time to buy them... a well-known watch-maker whom the Neuchâtel Museum employed to look after its clocks. And he gave her the man's name.

"Ah, there we are...!" said Claudine at her end of the line... "He has a lovely daughter..." Then, thinking that in the face of such convincing facts, I should make what she called a confession, she told me about her discovery.

"But I know the dear man," was all I answered. "Yet I assure you I know nothing about a daughter, lovely or not."

"Oh... go on!" shouted Claudine with a vulgarity which hurt.

"It's so true," I said crossly, "that we are going at once to telephone him and ask if he can give me, or rather give us, the key to this mystery."

Then, suddenly, the truth burst upon me and I began to roar with laughter.

"You're laughing on the wrong side of your mouth," cried Claudine, beside herself (and at that moment I noticed that she was not as pretty as

I had imagined). It took me some time to recover.

"No," I said, controlling myself at last. "Listen, Claudine . . . it is neither the great watch-maker nor his beautiful daughter who wrote these strange messages. All they did was to transmit them!"

"But who from?" asked Claudine with angry eyes that started out of her face like those of a lobster.

"They were composed by the watch-maker but actually written by . . . The Writer."

"The Writer? What Writer? What story are you inventing now?" muttered Claudine, as angry as ever.

"The Writer of Jaquet Droz. It's an automaton that looks like a little boy . . . this automaton, or, more exactly, this android, which caused such a commotion in the reign of Marie Antoinette and which has since been kept in the town museum beside The Musician (who plays the organ) and The Artist. These three automats become alive on the first of each month, to the great delight of visitors, and that explains why I always then received the amorous letters which The Writer executed with such care and elegance. Well . . . I helped to bring back some fame to this automaton, forgotten by our neighbours in France, by promoting his journey to Paris where, at the Museum of Arts and Crafts, he performed a thousand wonders for crowds of enthusiastic visitors. To thank me for my help in a really original way the curator of the museum sends me every month these 'autograph' messages bearing witness to the rather overwhelming gratitude of the mechanical Writer . . . and his own."

"But why repeat the messages so often?" asked Claudine, still suspicious.

"It's simple enough: I have several addresses; I travel enormously, and the messages were sent as a precaution in several copies to the four corners of the earth. It was only a joke, but your suspicion has turned the comedy into a tragedy and given it an importance that it ought never to have had."

"That's a better explanation!" said Claudine, calmer now (and alas! she again seemed to me to be quite charming).

Two weeks later I was at the Neuchâtel Museum, the only visitor that day, and I fell into contemplation before The Writer, back now in his place. I found him delightful, and the absence of any custodian

# THE LOVE-LETTER

left me free to make a rather childish gesture which amused me: I gave the chubby little artist a kiss (a "peck," as they say in my part of the world).

At that moment a sigh attracted my attention. Yet I was alone in the empty, echoing room. Then I found with amazement that The Writer's neighbour, The Musician, was breathing deeply, and from her came these heartbreaking sighs.

"She is in love with The Writer," I thought . . . "and jealous, like Claudine!"

A little shiver that the inexplicable provokes ran down my back, and it was with genuine relief that I saw the curator of the museum come into the room.

"Tell me, dear Sir," I said rather shyly, "am I the victim of an illusion or of too much of the good wine of Neuchâtel? But I have the impression that your Musician moves and sighs . . . !"

"You are quite right. A little while ago we demonstrated the talents of The Musician for the benefit of the Maharajah of Coroda. The mechanism which moves her fingers and that which works the breathing are controlled by two different springs. When the former has ceased to function, the latter remains in action for some time still to keep alive in the spectator's mind the illusion of life . . . a very striking illusion, don't you think?"

"Much too striking!" I said, relieved.

All the same, though I have burnt a great many letters in my life, I shall not destroy the love-letters written for me by a little boy more than a hundred and sixty years old. Is he not the only being in the world who could, a hundred years after my death, send me similar letters, just as carefully written, just as warmhearted, just as peremptory?

A month after that, crossing the Bahnhof Street in Zurich, I caught sight of the dancer, who recognised me and came to meet me. With the usual greetings I unfortunately took it into my head to return to the subject of his disclosure. I could not help telling him that it seemed better never to receive love-letters than to receive them, as had happened to me, from a robot.

"Robot!" exclaimed the dancer, to whom the word was new.

"Robot . . . automaton if you prefer," I answered.

I saw his expression change. "Excuse me," he muttered, looking at his wrist-watch, "but I have an awful lot to do."

"*Spokoinonotche* [good night]," he added, and without shaking my hand he hurriedly crossed the wide avenue, obviously anxious to put its whole width between him and me. Since that meeting he has never again been to see me.